"I have decided to start a little school for young ladies here in Crome," said Martha.

"You will do no such thing," said Drum. "You will not look after any more young ladies, because they are an ungrateful lot, and it is time that somebody looked after you." Gently he put his hands on her shoulders and turned her face towards himself.

"I am a very independent woman, Mr. Connington," Martha said firmly. "I like to stand on my own feet."

"Women have no right to be independent." He frowned and his hands dropped to his sides. "Martha, start your little school if you must, but I am not going to give up. I shall come back again and again, until one day I shall come as usual and I shall say, 'Now will you marry me?' And you will say—quite meekly—'Yes, please, Drum, I will.'"

Martha laughed. But her heart was racing with a strange excitement.

The
Tempestuous
Petticoat

Mary Ann Gibbs

A FAWCETT CREST BOOK • NEW YORK

For
PHILIP
with my thanks

THE TEMPESTUOUS PETTICOAT

THIS BOOK CONTAINS THE COMPLETE TEXT OF THE
ORIGINAL HARDCOVER EDITION.

Published by Fawcett Crest Books, CBS Publications, the
Consumer Publishing Division of CBS Inc., by arrangement
with Mason/Charter Publishers, Inc.

ISBN: 0-449-23489-4

Printed in the United States of America

10 9 8 7 6 5 4 3 2 1

One

The stage came down Crome High Street at a good pace, the April sun picking out its smart new paint and the scarlet coat of the guard, and flashing on the brass horn with which he was sounding his call.

The three young Lingfords watched its approach with a mixture of feelings: Martha the eldest with apprehension, her younger sister Sukey with pouting resignation, and their thirteen-year-old brother Charles with unconcealed excitement.

"I do wish," Miss Honeyman said, as it slackened speed in approaching the Bull Inn where her nieces and nephew were to join it, "I do wish, Martha dear, that you had not decided to travel in a road coach. Your papa would never have allowed it. He would have insisted on you all travelling in a chaise from the

Bull here. They are so clean and well kept and they have such good horses and postboys. You never know what the drivers of these dirty coaches are like—some of them get so drunk. Your papa always travelled by chaise: he would have been dreadfully distressed had he known you were to go this way."

"One has to cut one's garment to fit one's cloth," Martha said cheerfully. It would have taken two chaises to convey the three of them, their maid Betsy, and the luggage that had not been already despatched to Kent by the London wagon, and twenty miles at one and sixpence a mile for each chaise would have been far too costly under their present reduced circumstances. She did not remind her aunt that it was because their dear papa had lived consistently beyond his means that his children were now unable to afford the comfort of posting.

"I hope it is not an old coach," went on Miss Honeyman. "You cannot tell from the outside, dear. That new paint might be hiding a multitude of cracks. Your Uncle Josiah travelled by stage once years ago, when he was a young man, against his father's advice, and the bottom fell out when it was going downhill. He makes a joke of it now, but I know he did not think it a joke at the time."

"But dearest Aunt Deb, this is one of the new ones: You can see for yourself how splendid it looks, and there are a lot of passengers—at least a dozen outside. It would not carry nearly so many if it were unsafe."

"But it will take you much longer to get to Bath—at least four hours or more, with all the stops on the way."

"Never mind. We shall be going by the Mail from

Bath to London on Friday and we shall fly along then."

The great vehicle came to a stop with a rattling of hoofs, a jingling of harness and a creaking of wheels on the cobbles outside the inn, and after some of the passengers alighted, having reached the end of their journey, Miss Honeyman put her head inside to satisfy herself that it was not too dirty to receive her nieces new travelling cloaks, and voiced a suspicion that the straw on the floor might not have been changed very recently.

Charles having dodged round the steaming horses to beg for a seat beside the driver, then watched the disposal of their trunks in the boot with great cheerfulness, taking especial care that a portmanteau of his own was disposed of properly and not being so particular of his sisters' belongings.

"Aunt Deb is right, Martha," said Sukey after she had embraced her aunt tearfully and was preparing to get into the coach. "We ought to have had a chaise." She wrinkled her pretty nose: "It *smells*! And you know I am always sick if I do not sit with my back to the horses."

Whereupon an old gentleman, who had spread himself and his possessions over the seat in question after its last occupant had left the coach, hastily made room for her beside him.

"I must request you, however, not have the window open," he said, regarding her suspiciously over his spectacles. "It is very dangerous to have open windows in public conveyances."

"If I am sick I shall *have* to have the window open," Sukey said peevishly.

"But you said you were not sick when you sat with your back to the horses."

"I meant to say that I am not sick so often," explained Sukey.

Betsy was bundled inside, hung about with so many packages and parcels that she had to keep counting them to see that she had them all, in between admonishing Charles to keep his greatcoat on in case it rained. The pastrycook's wife, as fresh and wholesome as one of her husband's loaves, came out on the step of the stop next to the Bull to wave them goodbye, while James Brand, the bootmaker, who had made all their father's boots, touched his hat to them as he hurried by, the end of his measure poking out of his pocket. Then the last of the luggage was stored away, the last of the passengers helped up on top—the coach taking no more than six inside—the horses had been exchanged for fresh ones, and there was nothing to keep them any longer. Martha exchanged a last warm hug with her aunt and prepared to get in beside Betsy.

"Write to me, my dear," Miss Honeyman said, her eyes wet. "I wish you had heard from your grandfather. I do not like his silence, my love. You should have had a letter from him by now."

"But you know my Uncle Josiah says he never did write letters, dearest." Martha smiled at her reassuringly. "Do not worry about us, Aunt Deb. We shall manage splendidly." She climbed into the coach, the steps were removed, the door shut, the guard was up behind and they were off, the horn sounding gaily as they rattled through the streets of the little town, as if they could not part from it fast enough.

Martha felt a slight constriction of the throat as they

came out into open country on the Bath road, but her sister was busy untying the ribbons that fastened her cloak and spreading her skirts as far as she dared under the disapproving eyes of the old gentleman, while Charles from his seat beside the coachman was too pleased with his position and the rate at which they travelled to give another thought to the home they were leaving behind. He was at an age when the future spelt adventure at every new experience.

"Do you ever meet with any highwaymen on this road?" he asked. "I mean at night—not in broad daylight of course."

The coachman said there had not been any for the past few years. "And not only on this road neither," he added. "There don't seem to be so many of the gentry about these days."

"Now why do you think that is?" Charles felt slightly disappointed.

"People travel fast," said the coachman. "That's one reason. The Bath to London road used to be one of the worst for robbery, but since them machines hev come on the roads there's few as would risk trying to stop 'em. And another reason," he added with a solemn look at his young passenger, "may be a man's natural aversion to being 'anged, 'uman nature being what it is. There ain't much future in being 'anged, is there, sir?"

Charles wondered for a moment if he was being smoked and decided against it. He was no child, after all, being nearly fourteen. He said cheerfully, "I have never driven a four-in-hand, but I daresay four are as easy to handle as two."

"Would you say so indeed, sir?" The coachman's

solemn look had returned. "But you are accustomed to handling the reins no doubt?"

"I drove my father's carriage from time to time," Charles said loftily. Carriage was perhaps rather too grand a term for Captain Lingford's little pleasure cart, but it sounded a great deal better.

"And that would be a pair of horses, sir?" said the coachman.

Charles was forced to admit that his father had only kept one horse. "But a team like this would not be difficult to drive," he added.

"That depends," said the coachman. "The last man we had on this run what said that had a most unfortunate accident the day after he joined us. Mind you, he was . . ." He paused.

"Bosky?" suggested Charles.

"Exactly so, sir." Having reached a broad and level stretch of the turnpike, the coachman gave a little encouraging jerk of the reins and the horses gathered speed. "We gave him a good funeral, and each of us drivers had a pair o' gloves, which was generous considering he'd only been with us two days."

Charles did not feel inclined to discuss funerals.

"I daresay you know your horses very well?" he said.

"Know 'em, sir? I know 'em as I know my own children and better, since I see more of 'em."

When they changed horses again he appeared to know that four equally well, and even a third lot that were to take them into Bath held no problems for him, although he had some scathing things to say about the off-leader.

"Nasty-tempered brute if ever there was one," he

told Charles, scowling at the animal's ears. "Fell down in the middle of Bath last week and it took six of us to sit on 'im afore we could git 'im on 'is legs again. Did it apurpose."

"Did he hurt himself?" asked Charles.

" 'Urt himself? *That* critter? No, he just did it out of contrariness. A most contrary animal, is that."

Charles's thoughts left the off-leader and went to his grandfather. According to his father in the old days the old gentleman had a stable full at Emmetts. No doubt he would let his grandson take his pick of them, and before long he would have learnt how to drive a four-in-hand, which, in spite of his companion on the box, he did not think could be very difficult.

They dined on the way and arrived in Bath at eight, and Charles was relieved when they parted from the coach and its team, the off-leader's eye beginning to roll ominously as they came down the street to the coach office.

Their uncle, Mr. Josiah Honeyman, had sent his carriage for them, and a servant was there with a handcart for their luggage. Mr. Honeyman was the eldest of the four children of an attorney in Tonbridge in Kent and having no desire to work for a living, at the age of twenty-one he had courted and won a woman with a fortune of thirty thousand pounds, a large house in Bath and a smaller one in a fashionable quarter of London. Having thus assured himself of a comfortable income, he was able to combine his natural habit of indolence with kindly gossip over dinner tables at which he ate and drank a great deal more than was good for him.

His sister Alicia had been an extremely pretty girl

and at one of the monthly assemblies in Tonbridge she had attracted the admiration of Captain Vincent Lingford, the only surviving child of Henry Lingford of Emmetts Hall in Kent. The young man's admiration had turned to love and he had married pretty Alicia in the face of violent opposition from his father, who had refused to acknowledge his son's existence thereafter.

Josiah thereupon wrote to his younger brother John, who had followed his father's profession and was now a struggling attorney in London, suggesting that he should write to Mr. Lingford and request him to mend his ways.

John dutifully wrote, and having received no reply to a number of letters, in response to a further request from Josiah, situated comfortably in Bath, spent money he could ill afford in travelling to Emmetts to see the gentleman in person. He saw him for a brief few minutes, during which Mr. Lingford informed him that if he ever set foot in the place again he would set the dogs on him, which was not an encouraging way of conducting family business.

Now, however, with both Alicia and her devoted Vincent dead, John Honeyman had taken it upon himself to write once more to Mr. Henry Lingford, hoping that the years might have softened his heart.

He reminded him that he was the only relative to whom his grandchildren could turn for assistance, and suggested that they should journey to Kent and make their home with him at the end of April. He ended by saying that if he did not hear to the contrary he would conclude that they would be received at Emmetts Hall.

After two months had passed without a reply the attorney set things in train for the three young people to remove from Crome to Kent. He concluded that old Lingford had probably regretted his treatment of his son and was too proud to admit it—that, in short, silence gave consent.

With his usual indolence Josiah Honeyman left such matters to his brother to arrange, being encouraged by his wife Sophia, who was quick to point out that they had two daughters of their own to marry off without offering hospitality to pretty nieces, while, as for Charles, boys could always make their way in the world without any help from anyone.

Having thus quietened his conscience and stilled any slight desire he might feel to exert himself, Josiah invited the young Lingfords to stay a few nights in Bath before travelling on to London and then to Kent. Neither prospect was very pleasing to Martha. At twenty-two she was looked on by her sister and brother as being the mentor of the family, but she did not forget the pitying looks of their Aunt Sophia on the one occasion when she had visited them in Crome, and she remembered resentfully their cousins' old gowns that had been sent to swell her own and Sukey's wardrobes after her visit. It had given her immense pleasure to give them to Betsy to be cut up for her sister's children.

She hoped they would not have to meet many of her aunt's friends in Bath, and planned to spend days in sightseeing should anything have been arranged for their entertainment. And she tried to forget that when they left Bath they still had the ordeal of meeting an unfeeling old man who had not troubled to write to them when his only son died.

The situation was one, however, that Martha was

prepared to meet with her usual spirit, because Sukey
was the image of their mother and quite the prettiest
girl anybody had set eyes on in years, and she had not
the slightest doubt that sooner or later she must meet
a rich man who would fall in love with her and marry
her. Sukey needed pretty dresses and fine jewels and
carriages and servants and an adoring husband, where
others—ordinary folk like herself—could do very well
without them. It was Sukey who had to be cherished
and loved and looked after and cared for, not only
because she was so pretty but because such things
would not spoil her. Martha had been indignant when,
in discussing her sister with her aunt one day, Miss
Honeyman had suggested that dearest Sukey was just
a mite spoiled already.

They arrived in Bath at eight o'clock in time for
supper with their uncle, who apologized for the absence of their Aunt Sophia and their cousins. They had
gone to a ball, he told them, almost the last ball of the
season in the Upper Rooms.

The young Lingfords were glad to be alone with
their uncle. They spent a pleasant few hours with him
and when Martha thanked him again for his hospitality
he said in his good-natured way that it would do them
good to stay a little while and walk about the streets
of Bath and see the shops there and go to the theatre
or a ball.

As they had no money to spend in the shops and
as she and Sukey were in mourning for their father and
had no suitable ball-gowns, while Charles had no
knowledge of dancing and trod frequently on his
partners' toes, they were relieved to discover next
morning that the only festivity their aunt had arranged

for them was an evening party, to drink coffee and tea at Lady Wintersham's in Sydney Place.

Admiral Sir Thomas Wintersham had lately retired from the sea and as several of his old shipmates had retired to Bath, he had chosen to join them there, and it seemed to Charles that it was a lucky chance that was to take them to his house in Sydney Place that evening. Next to driving a four-in-hand his great ambition was to go into the Navy. Once secure of a ship, he told his uncle, he had no doubt that he would win a great deal of prize money and be able to support his sisters in luxury for the rest of their lives.

"Then you'll have to do better than our Navy appears to be doing at present," said Josiah indulgently. "The balance in prizes seems to be in favour of the French."

In the meantime he suggested that they should walk out with him, their aunt and cousins refusing to accompany them, pleading fatigue from the ball, which they abused as being extremely dull.

"A dull ball is so much more fatiguing than any other," Mrs. Honeyman said. "And it was a very dull ball last night. I quite wished you and Sukey had been there to add to the numbers. Nothing can be duller than a few couples standing up by themselves in a large room."

As the only balls Martha had attended had been held in the small Assembly Rooms at Crome, where more than a dozen couples could be too many, she felt she was in no position to offer an opinion, and they went off alone with their uncle, Martha walking ahead with him while Charles followed with Sukey.

"I believe your grandfather has a very large house

in Kent?" Mr. Honeyman remarked as they started out.

"I have always understood it to be so," Martha agreed. Her father had told her that Emmetts Hall had been built in the days of Elizabeth and was the most beautiful house he had ever seen.

"And a great deal of land too perhaps?" said Mr. Honeyman.

"At least a thousand acres I believe, sir."

Her Uncle Josiah said that he was very glad that their future was so well assured. "There is a gentleman from Kent, a Mr. Meldrum Connington, who is visiting Bath at this moment and I believe he knows your grandfather. It is a pity your stay here is to be so short or you might have met him."

Martha said she would like to meet him. "But I am afraid there will be no time as we leave on Friday," she added regretfully. She was, however, to meet Mr. Connington in spite of it.

They had stopped at a stationer's in Milsom Street where Charles bought his elder sister a lady's pocket book for 1794, reduced in price from two shillings to sixpence because the year was well advanced, and as they came out they stopped to look in at a print-shop window where there were a number of pictures of ships, among them some of naval vessels. As the four of them were examining them a gentleman stopped to greet their uncle and be introduced.

Mr. Meldrum Connington was a tall man with a lean face and dark hair that he wore cut short *à la Titus*. He was fashionably dressed and there was something of the dandy about him, the trousers that he wore in place of breeches—trousers being *haut ton*—being so skin-tight that Charles wondered how he could sit down in them. His cravat was tied without a crease, he wore light-coloured gloves and carried a cane, and his jewelled watch-chain bore a cluster of gold seals.

He raised his quizzing glass to study Mr. Honeyman's companions with some astonishment. He had the air of a man to whom life has become somewhat of a bore. Martha judged him to be all of thirty and took an instant dislike to him: no man as well-to-do as Mr. Connington appeared to be had any right to be bored.

"My nieces and nephew are travelling to Kent to make their home with their grandfather, Mr. Henry Lingford," Josiah told him. "I believe he is a neighbour of your father's at Meldrum, so that I daresay you will have met him frequently?"

"Mr. Henry Lingford?" Mr. Connington dropped his glass to brush a speck of dust from the sleeve of his exquisitely cut green coat. "I believe I may have seen the old gentleman out in his little cart sometimes when I have been staying at Meldrum, but I do not recollect ever having spoken to him in my life."

"I daresay my grandfather uses a closed carriage more often than he did," Martha said crisply, annoyed by the patronizing way in which he had referred to the "little cart" and disliking his affected drawl. "He is well over seventy years of age."

"If he has a closed carriage, he keeps it well hidden," said Mr. Connington, his drawl slightly more pronounced. "I have never seen it. But that is not to say," he added, seeing her flush, "that he has not got one in his stables. The fact is, Mr. Honeyman," he went on turning back to her uncle, "Mr. Lingford does not entertain his friends very frequently, and neither does he like dining abroad. My father pays him a morning call about twice a year, I believe, and Mr. Lingford returns the compliment by sending him fish that has been caught in the bay when it occurs to him to do so, and there the acquaintance ends." His cool grey eyes dwelt for a moment on pretty Sukey, and from her they went back to Martha and noted the resentment in her face with a flicker of interest. Very few young ladies showed resentment on being noticed by Drum Connington. "But now that he is to have young relatives about him no doubt things will be widely different." He bowed and raising his hat he wished them a pleasant journey and walked on.

"He evidently does not know my grandfather as well as you fancied, Uncle," Martha said, still mortified by the reference to the little cart, and she added that she did not think that Mr. Connington's acquaintance with the old gentleman went beyond his father's morning visits.

"I daresay that is very true, my dear," said her uncle placidly. "Mr. Meldrum Connington was left an estate in Gloucestershire through the death of a cousin some years ago and he spends more time at his charming little house—Arcott Manor—than he does at Meldrum in Kent. He is a very wealthy young man, I believe. I would not take it at all amiss if he were to have a fancy for one of my girls."

"He is not married then?"

"Oh no, my dear."

"And has he shown a preference for either of my cousins?"

"He has not." Her uncle sighed. "It is said by his friends that Drum Connington is hard to please."

Martha's dislike for the man grew: it appeared that he was conceited as well, though one would have guessed as much from the way he studied one through that ridiculous glass.

No doubt every girl in Bath was striving for his attention. She was sorry they were not staying longer in the city so that she could show him there was one young lady who did not care if he noticed her or not.

Two

Drum Connington strolled on to Gay Street where one of his married sisters had taken a house for three months, her husband being attacked by gout and ordered by his physician to drink the waters there, and as he walked his mind dwelt with some amusement on the dark-haired young woman who had flown into a pet because of his remarks about her grandfather. But had she never met the old man? he wondered. Did she not know what an old renegade he was?

His own father, Sir William Connington, with other justices of the peace in the district, found Mr. Lingford extremely embarrassing at times. It was only a little while ago that a charge had been brought against him by the Customs officials in Rydd, the little seaport and fishing town five miles from Meldrum. Not that anyone ever took a great deal of notice of charges brought by

Customs officials and there could scarcely be a soul in Rydd who was not connected with the smuggling of contraband in some way. And now that the French refused to allow English goods to be imported no doubt trade of that kind might be on the increase.

It had been rumoured for some time, however, that Mr. Lingford was the owner of a cutter that was used ostensibly for fishing and was in fact known to be employed for trading in contraband, and although nobody in Rydd would ever be persuaded to give evidence against the old man, Sir William had recently paid him a morning call in order to utter a timely warning.

When his son asked later how he had taken it his father replied ruefully that the old devil had merely given one of his wicked grins and said he would drink his health in the next lot of French brandy to come his way.

And that was the old man to whom these three young people were going, in all innocence, foreseeing a pleasant home with an ageing relative. He wondered how they would fare, and he thought in particular of the girl Josiah Honeyman called Martha. He fancied that she might be a match for her grandfather, and he thought idly that it might be worth his while to pay a visit to Meldrum later on, to discover for himself how the young Lingfords were progressing.

Having arrived at the lodgings in Gay Street and been admitted to his sister's drawing-room on the first floor, he endured her warm salutation and returned it with a languid if brotherly kiss.

"I do not think I like this fashion for short hair," she said, standing back and regarding him critically. "Yours has always curled naturally—though why the only boy of the family should have curling hair while his six sisters' hair was all as straight as a rat's tail is a mystery I have never been able to fathom. But because it curls, of course, short hair does become you."

"Thank you, my dear." He bowed. "Compliments are rare from you, Fanny."

"I speak my mind, Drum, and while you remain unmarried I shall continue to do so. The barber who came this morning wished to give Edmund the guillotine, but he resolutely refused."

"I should think so indeed. It is a barbarous fashion —hair cut neither short nor long, ragged and unkempt, and worn with a narrow scarlet ribbon round the neck."

"Drum!" She was horrified. "I did not realize—and neither did Edmund, I am sure. How can men be so heartless and so odious for the sake of setting a new and stupid fashion? Does nobody remember that there are scores of French *émigrés* over here?"

Drum examined a well-manicured hand with some care. "It would be difficult to forget them, my dear. They swarm in London like flies in hot weather."

"I hope you will be careful what you say about them when you are next at Meldrum. Papa has invited an old friend, M. de Salle, and his family to stay there as long as they please. But, of course, they will have to escape from France first and I daresay that will be difficult."

"I should say they will succeed if the revolutionaries across the water have left them enough money."

How cynical he was getting, she thought regretfully. There was a brittleness, a total lack of heart, about the young men of today, and every time she met her brother she seemed to detect a new cynicism, a fresh brittleness, that made 'her unhappy for him. What he needed more than ever was a wife to teach him kind-ness and gentleness again. He had been the dearest brother in the world until Anna Duffington had become his mistress, enslaving him with her beauty and threat-ening to ruin him with the ruthless greed of her de-mands.

"Are you coming with me to the Wintershams' to-night?" she asked more cheerfully. "Lady Wintersham was very particular in asking you. The two Miss Honeymans are to be there."

"Then I will visit Edmund and play chess with him instead."

"Janet, who is not yet out, has promised to play chess with her father, but if I am to have no escort he will be forced to accompany me."

"What! And have him standing about all evening with that gouty knee? You could not be so cruel."

"But if you will not come what am I to do?"

"You are indeed in a quandary," he agreed amiably.

She could have boxed his ears. She said brightly that she was sorry for Mrs. Honeyman. "She has some young relatives staying with them for a few days," she told him. "They arrived too late—or were too tired—to come to the ball in the Upper Rooms last night, but I was told by a mutual acquaintance that the younger niece is extremely pretty and that if she had been plain no doubt they would have been there. They are to be at the Wintershams' tonight."

"In that case I will be happy to escort you," her brother said, relenting. "Any pretty face that has not been seen in Bath this last twelvemonth is worth a scrutiny."

But it was not of Sukey that he was thinking.

The evening party in Sydney Place proved to be entertaining as well as helpful to the young Lingfords. No sooner did Admiral Wintersham discover that Charles was anxious to go to sea than he took him into the back drawing-room where a dozen or so drawings of the old ships in which he had served were displayed on the walls, and he related many stories of the battles in which he had taken part, and the dangers he had encountered in foreign ports, and the prizes he had brought home. He was delighted by the interest the lad showed and when Martha joined them he told her that he thought her grandfather could not do better than to approach the Admiralty and enquire if their lordships would take him at the Royal Navy School in Portsmouth.

"Your brother tells me that he will be fourteen in July," he said. "So that there is not much time to lose. The school takes boys from eleven years of age to fifteen, and if I were to write their lordships a letter to be enclosed in that of your grandfather's I am pretty sure they would not refuse to take him. Later there would be a further training period of three years at sea, and his captain would see that he did a certain amount of desk work, like map reading and so on. I believe he would take to it as readily as my boy did."

Martha said that she would be very grateful to have a letter from him to send to their lordships of the Admiralty and he promised that she should have it before they left Bath on Friday. Then he took them into the front drawing-room where a number of people had collected and introduced them to his youngest son, a lieutenant in the Royal Navy. His eyes were immediately captured by Sukey, and certainly Martha thought fondly, their cousins in their fashionable dresses and jewels looked nothing beside her lovely little sister in her white cambric muslin and black ribbons.

The young man allowed his attention to be taken from her for a few moments in which to tell Charles that he would find the school in Portsmouth a grind, but that a great many good fellows went to it, and at the end of a year he would find himself scampering about a ship's rigging like a monkey. And then he returned to Sukey's bright eyes and engaging smiles.

Martha observed to her annoyance that Mr. Connington was there and that he stationed himself near enough to her sister to listen to her nonsense with a faint smile, and presently he moved nearer to herself and said, "I understand that you were not at the ball last night, Miss Lingford?"

"No." And then fearful lest the brevity of the reply sounded rude she added quickly that they had arrived too late to go to it.

"I congratulate you," he said with the languid air that she had so disliked that morning. "It was a dead bore."

"You do not like dancing, Mr. Connington?"

"I detest it."

"Then why do you go to balls?"

"Why *does* one go to balls, indeed? Or, for the matter of that, to breakfasts and receptions and dinners? In order, I suppose, to pass the time."

"You find that difficult, Mr. Connington?" She spoke with a crispness that brought his eyes swiftly to her face. "I pity you indeed. It is hard for a gentleman of your years to be forced to such extremities. What will you be like when you are old?"

"That," he assured her, "is a contingency that has never entered my mind. But I will think about it, Miss Lingford." He bowed slightly, stayed a moment more to listen to Sukey, and in fact seemed once almost about to join in her conversation with James Wintersham and thought better of it, and joined the Honeyman girls and Miss Wintersham in the group round the piano.

Later that night as they got ready for bed Martha asked her sister if he had spoken to her at all.

"Mr. Connington? Oh, you mean that black-haired man who is Uncle Josiah's friend. I think he said it was a warm evening and I agreed and that was about all the conversation we had."

"You had a great deal more to say to the Admiral's son." Martha sounded a little uneasy. As James Wintersham was the Admiral's fourth son, he was not likely to have money enough to marry on for a number of years.

Sukey laughed. "Did my conversation with Lieutenant Wintersham worry you? Then let me put your mind at rest. I have no intention of pursuing that young man with any idea of matrimony. It would be no good if I had," she added with another laugh, "as he is joining his ship in the Downs next week while I shall be in Kent."

"You were flirting with him abominably," Martha said, trying to be severe.

"Exactly. Flirting. And there was no more in it than that as we both very well knew." Sukey pulled her nightshift over her head. "Don't be cross, Martha dear. There were a number of old ladies there this evening all eyes and ears. Think what an entertainment it must have been for them to watch me flirting with Lieutenant Wintersham. Cannot you hear them talking about me tomorrow? 'You should have seen the Honeymans' niece, my dear. A brazen hussy. What a good thing she is not staying long!' "

"Oh, Sukey!" Martha could not help laughing too. "What a lot of nonsense you talk. But you must recollect that you are no longer at school. You are grown up now, my love. You may laugh as much as you like but the time will soon come when you will be thinking seriously of getting married."

"But don't drive me into matrimony," Sukey said, pouting. "You are getting as bad as Aunt Deb, who saw a husband for me in every young man in Crome. I want someone a great deal more romantic than a farmer's son or a curate—or even a penniless lieutenant—when I marry, Martha, my husband must be rich as well as handsome."

Martha agreed that he must be rich and as they got into bed her thoughts turned from prospective husbands for Sukey to the journey to Kent and the meeting with their grandfather.

What would he be like, she wondered? Mr. Connington's talk about his "little cart" had puzzled and worried her, and it was when Sukey had mentioned Emmetts that he had frowned and looked as if he were about to break into her conversation with James Wintersham. It was as if he had known something about Emmetts that they did not know and that for a moment he wished to enlighten them before his customary languor returned and he walked across the room to the pianoforte, probably dismissing the young

Lingfords and their problems as being too great a bore
with which to concern himself.

She wished it had not been so, unreasonably, because she had not been over-polite to him herself. She
wished too that he had been less fine in his dress and
his manners. His evening waistcoat of white cashmere
had been heavily embroidered in triple silks, his snuff-
box had been of gold, his quizzing glass of gold instead
of the morning silver. The man was not only rich but
spoiled and not the type to whom one could turn for
information or advice.

In the large and luxurious bedroom below Mrs.
Honeyman said that she thought it strange that Martha
had received no reply to her letter to her grandfather
and was not reassured when her husband reminded
her that his brother had not received replies to any
letters he had written to the old gentleman in the past.

"I daresay he is not as rich as Martha seems to
think," went on Sophia, "but that is no reason why he
should not have the civility to answer letters." She
added after a moment: "Lady Wintersham's sister,
Miss Moss, told me in confidence that the stories she
had heard about him in the past were of the most un-
savoury character. She has a brother living down that
way."

"Henry Lingford is older now," Josiah said easily.
"Bless my soul, my dear, he is over seventy. I have
no doubt at all that he will have become sober in his
old age."

"I hope he has, because according to Miss Moss's
brother he was seldom sober in the old days. In fact
she said that her brother was always surprised that a
man like that could have such a nice fellow as poor
Vincent for a son. She was very sorry to hear of his

death. Have you been able to ascertain what money he left his children?"

"Martha told me that after the debts had been paid —he was never a frugal man—and the furniture and books had been sold to meet them, three hundred pounds was all that remained."

"And that is all they have in the world? One hundred pounds apiece?" Sophia was horrified.

"That is all they have, my dear." Nothing it seems could shake Mr. Honeyman's placidity.

"Then it is plainly the *duty* of their grandfather to support them all and to give them a home," said Mrs. Honeyman decidedly.

Her husband was only too happy to agree with her, although on the Friday evening, as he waved goodbye to his nieces and nephew on the London post coach from Bath, he could not help recollecting that duty was a word to which Mr. Henry Lingford had never taken kindly. But no doubt his brother John would have heard from him, he thought, as the coach moved off: he could safely leave everything to John.

Drum Connington, making his way to Gloucestershire in the following week, found his thoughts going back more than once to that evening at the Wintershams and in particular dwelling on Martha Lingford.

Dressed in mourning that did not become her, her eyes had held a directness and her mouth and chin a firmness that were undeniable. There was no beauty there, perhaps, but there was a strength of purpose sufficient to meet any opposition she might encounter from her grandfather. But he wished he had been able to tell her, as he listened to her sister's chatter about Emmetts, that the place no longer existed, that Henry Lingford had sold his house and estates years ago to settle the debts that had swallowed his entire fortune.

If her reception of him had not been so snappish he would have tried to find an opportunity of speaking to her again before the party ended, but her manner had been enough to dispel his concern for her family, and as he bowled along in his fine new carriage towards Arcott Manor he determined to dismiss her from his mind.

Let the young lady face her own problems: from the little he had seen of her he thought she would not thank anyone for trying to help her. In fact he felt his sympathy go out to old Lingford for the tempestuous petticoat that was about to invade his household.

The Bath mail left at eight and the Lingfords travelled overnight with lights until the moon got up. They arrived at the Angel in St. Clements punctually at eleven the next morning, on a fresh and beautiful April day.

There were only five inside passengers, Martha and Sukey, Betsy and two maiden ladies who had joined them at Devizes. The road had been good, the coach swift and their journey uneventful and comfortable. Martha had managed to sleep for a part of the time and Sukey had done the same, and although Betsy had said she would not close her eyes she had been snoring her head off on Martha's shoulder for the best part of six hours. As the steps were lowered and she followed the four ladies she looked about her anxiously for Charles, but, swinging down lightly from the top, he had no mind to be followed about the yard by his sisters' maid, who never let him forget that she had once been his nurse and he was making sure that all their luggage was unloaded.

Having tipped the guard and paid twelve shillings for their luggage, Martha looked about her for John Honeyman who was to meet them there, and saw him hurrying towards them.

"You are exactly on time," he told them as he kissed the girls and held out his hand to Charles. "It is wonderful how these new machines manage to keep to their timetables. They are scarcely ever late, and with the miles they cover it is quite astonishing. Did you have a comfortable journey?"

"Very comfortable, thank you, Uncle John." They had travelled at such a speed that Martha felt bruised all over from being flung about the carriage, but that was due to Betsy's unyielding parcels and baskets rather than the action of the coach. She could not think what she had put into them that made the bundles so hard and uncompromising.

Their uncle had ordered breakfast and in a very little while they were seated at a table in a private room attacking tea and coffee and cold tongue. As they ate he told them that he had engaged their rooms for two nights. "You said you wanted to see some of our London sights while you were here," he added with a smile for Sukey and Charles. "And that you want to go to the theatre tomorrow night."

"And Betsy will like to visit her sister in Hackney," added Martha. "Is it far out of London?"

"Not more than three miles. A Hackney coach will take her there and back, but I believe the fare is all of two shillings."

Martha said she would pay the fare. "I have quite a lot of money left from the sale of the furniture," she told him, smiling. "My father's books made sixty pounds and my pianoforte made eight, and the dining-table twelve and our beds five pounds apiece." She was determined to be cheerful and he did not wish to say anything that would dampen their spirits, and as he remained silent she asked with a touch of anxiety if he had heard from their grandfather.

He wished he could say that he had.

"Aunt Deb says that he never answered letters in the old days," Martha said. "I daresay there are many people like that. They say they will write tomorrow, you know, and then when tomorrow comes it is the next day, or else next week, or when they have a moment to spare, and the moment never comes."

"Fortunately an attorney's letters are usually answered with promptness," John Honeyman said dryly. He was very uneasy about the old man's continued silence, and he wished heartily that he had risked being set on by the Emmett dogs and gone down to see for himself. But it was too late now, and he asked cheerfully what they wanted to see first. "I am at your disposal until three o'clock when your aunt wishes you to dine with us," he said.

Charles wanted to see the Leverian Museum if it was not too far. "The Admiral said it was very interesting," he told him.

"It is just over Blackfriars Bridge, certainly not too far to walk and it is worth a visit, if only for the curiosities on show there."

"What sort of curiosities, sir?" Sukey would rather have visited some of the warehouses and shops.

"Birds, shells, fossils of all kinds, my dear. Savage costumes too, and weapons."

"Weapons?" Charles's eyes sparkled. "Then the museum it is!"

They left Betsy to dispose of their luggage and to

unpack what they would require in London and walked out with their uncle, returning with him to dine in his house in Newgate Street: a tall, narrow house that seemed a great deal too small for his family of seven little boys and girls.

Their aunt greeted them as warmly as their uncle had done and the dinner was plain, without any of the side dishes thought to be so necessary in Bath, but they enjoyed it a great deal more. Their Aunt Sophia had given the girls the name of her mantua-maker in London before they left, but to Sukey's disgust Martha said she had no money to spare for clothes.

London to the two younger Lingfords was the most exciting and interesting place in the world, and Martha caught some of their enthusiasm, allowing herself to forget for a time their more pressing problems as she visited St. James's' and the Tower to see the menagerie there, and went to the New Drury Lane Theatre on their second evening to see two very charming pieces performed there, Mrs. Jordan taking one of the principal parts.

They were up early on the following morning in order to see some more of the town before catching the coach that left for Tonbridge at eleven.

"You will have time to dine at Tonbridge," their uncle told them as he saw them off, "while you wait for the stage coach that will take you on to Rydd." A chaise could be hired from Rydd to take them out to Emmetts. He took Martha aside for a few moments to press five guineas into her hand.

"I wish I could give you more, my love," he said, not letting her think that the gift had been hard to find. "But if things should not be all that you anticipate—if, for some reason, your grandfather is unable to take you into his house—remember that there is a home for you all with me. Your aunt and I will be most happy to accommodate you, never think that we shall not. I could not let you go today without such an assurance, my love. I would not have known a happy moment had I not done so."

Martha thought of the house in Newgate Street and the rooms that were already filled with her uncle's family, she looked at his shabby clothes and thread-bare coat, and his thin, anxious but loving face, and contrasted it with the lack of any such assurances in Bath, and for the first time since she had set out on the journey from Somerset she felt tears pressing at the back of her eyes. He was so kind that she had no doubt that he meant what he said. However full his house might be, room would be made for the three of them in it cheerfully, without ever letting them think that they might be crowding his own family or their aunt. She kissed him gratefully.

"I shall not forget," she said. "I promise you that if we are ever in trouble, dearest Uncle John, I will turn to you first of all."

And then he let her go.

Three

April was nearing its end, but just to make sure that they knew which month they were in, showers met them as they left London behind and continued until they reached Tonbridge, when the sun came out and all the primroses opened like bouquets in the hedges.

From Tonbridge the stage took them on through a gentle countryside where oaks were showing gold against the green, and willows hung yellow strands over ponds and streams.

It was nearly half past seven when they came in sight of Rydd Castle standing at the top of the line of hills two or three miles ahead.

The castle had been built to command not only the harbour but the marsh to east and west of the town, when in the old days the marauding French had come to sack and plunder and murder the inhabitants of the town, a habit that the English of those days had been quick to imitate on the other side of the Channel.

After the first thrill of seeing the castle and knowing that their journey was nearly at an end, Martha looked about her eagerly for Emmetts Hall. It was on the west side of the road, Captain Lingford had said, as you approached from Tonbridge, but although the castle was getting clearer every moment she could see nothing of Emmetts and concluded that it must be hidden behind trees that had grown up since their father's day. It was, after all, nearly twenty-five years since Captain Lingford had left home for the last time.

The house stood back, he had said, in a park, but the only house she could see in a park was a large white modern building, with a lake in front and a winding road up to it, the entrance from the Tonbridge road being flanked by two neat lodges on either side of impressive gates of massive wrought iron.

Maybe they had come by a different road than the one their father had known, and when they arrived at their destination in Rydd they would find a chaise from Emmetts waiting for them there.

They reached the top of the hill at a snail's pace, the loaded coach taking its time, but as they came abreast of the castle they were able to see the shape of the town below, as neatly contained as if its walls still stood against the French, the marsh spreading out into the distance to east and west and the blue circle of the sea reaching to the horizon to the south.

Brakes were applied, shoes being slipped under the wheels, the guard got down from his seat and went to the leaders' heads, discouraging them from going too

fast down into the town as energetically as the coachman had been encouraging them to pull up on the other
side. And indeed the cobbled streets were so narrow,
the overhanging storeys of the house so close, that the
greatest care was needed if some of the outside passengers were not to be knocked senseless or decapitated
before they reached the George Inn in the town square.

The George was a very large rambling old building
on the south side of the square opposite the Town Hall.
There was a notice outside stating that post-chaises
could be hired for any distance at any time of the day
or night, and as they got out of the coach and stretched
their cramped limbs, Martha looked about her for the
chaise that should have been sent to take them on to
Emmetts, but it seemed that if her grandfather had
received her letter he had forgotten that they were to
arrive that day.

The church clock was striking eight and with some
anxiety she asked the landlord for a chaise to take
them out to Emmetts. "Maybe we shall need two," she
added, with a glance at the luggage that surrounded
them.

"Emmetts, miss?" The landlord seemed genuinely
puzzled. "But there ain't no such place hereabouts. Not
now, that is."

"But that is nonsense." She was annoyed by the stu-
pidity of the Kent rustics. "You must know Emmetts
Hall. It is where my grandfather lives—Mr. Henry
Lingford."

His brow cleared and he laughed. "Lor' bless you,
my dear, Mr. Lingford don't live at Emmetts no more.
He sold it to Sir George Racksby must be all of ten
year ago. Sir George he pulled down the old place and

built a fine new house on the hill where it stood. He calls it Racksby Place. You must hev seen it as you come by on the Tonbridge road."

"Yes," said Martha hollowly. "I saw it." That brash new house with its square whiteness of stone, the long sash windows opening to the ground, the parapet with the stone figures in the Greek style that was so popular with rich men of taste these days. "Where then," she asked, "does my grandfather live now?" She had a bad moment when she thought he might tell her that he was dead, but he laughed again.

"Why he lives here in Rydd, my dear," he said. "Leastways a mile or so outside the town. You can walk it easy."

"As we have a quantity of luggage that will scarcely be possible." Martha felt her temper rising. "I should be obliged if you will have a carriage made ready for us at once."

"Certainly, miss. I'll have the horses put to this moment." The man shot a curious glance at the three young people and their servant before disappearing into the stable-yard, and in a very short while the only coach that the inn possessed appeared.

"If 'twon't take all your luggage you can leave some of it here," he told Martha. "It'ull be safe 'nough till Mr. Lingford sends for it tomorrow or somewhen."

They agreed that this would be the best plan and they got into the carriage, Charles once more riding with the coachman with what luggage that could be accommodated piled behind him and about his feet.

They rattled down the street towards a massive arch that had formed the west gate to the town in the days when it was a walled city, and they came out on to a flat desolate road across the marsh, the smell of the sea about them, and the shadows of the evening beginning to spread across the land to the south, gulls crying plaintively overhead.

It seemed to Martha that they were leaving all habitation and shelter behind: here and there a small hedge would rise from the ditches that lined the road and at one point a thicket threw deep and menacing shadows across it, and then they were out again and on the open road, with a cluster of wind-swept trees ahead and a tall red-brick house in the midst of them.

The house was three storeys high: it had a high wall in front, enclosing an overgrown courtyard, and as the carriage stopped and they got out in the fading light they saw that the iron gates were fastened with a padlocked chain.

Grass and nettles grew rankly round the base of the gates as if they had not been opened for a long time, the brick piers to which they were attached green with lichen and moss, while one of the stone pineapples that had adorned the top of the piers was lying on its side in the nettles.

Beyond the courtyard the windows of the house were shuttered and some of the slates in the shallow roof had come adrift. It was not a house that promised a welcome.

Telling her brother and sister to stay with Betsy, Martha turned to the gates, looking for a bell to pull to summon a servant to open them, when the coachman told her that nobody had opened them in years.

"Then how do you suggest that I should approach the front door?" she demanded.

He grinned uneasily and said there was a side gate

and a path indicating its direction with his whip. She found the gate under a screen of ivy: it was open and she marched up the overgrown path to the door. The steps were unswept, the bell handle rusty from lack of use, and with all her inherent prejudice against her grandfather uppermost she pulled it angrily, following it up with a sharp rat-tat with the iron knocker.

After a while a flickering light appeared behind the fanlight and she heard bolts being drawn back. The door opened a crack to reveal a manservant with a candle in his hand, while behind him a shrill female voice asked who was there.

"Never mind who is here," Martha said, now so angry and dismayed at what might lay in front of her brother and sister as well as herself that she was unable to pick her words. "Open the door and take me to Mr. Lingford at once."

The door opened wider and as she stepped into the hall a woman with her face heavily painted tried to bar the way.

"Who are you?" she demanded roughly. "And what does the likes of you want with the master?"

"That is my business," Martha told her crisply, "and his." She waited for the servant to take her to her grandfather and for a moment she thought the woman might be going to attack her, and then a door to the right opened and a voice asked who the devil was there at this time of night, and what the hell did they want?

Martha turned her head and in the lighted doorway she saw her grandfather for the first time: a short, stout old man, unshaven and with dirty white hair over a dirtier shirt. His feet were thrust into scuffed slippers, his breeches were worn and greasy and unbuttoned at the knees, and his whole aspect was in fact so revolting to her senses that she recoiled instinctively.

"*You?*" she said with disgust. "Are you Mr. Henry Lingford?"

"And what if I am? Who the devil are you?"

"I regret to say that I am your grand-daughter." Her head went up as she remembered Mr. Meldrum Connington's remarks about the old man and his father's slight acquaintance with him. What gentleman in Sir William Connington's position would wish to pay one morning call a year on such a man and in such a house? "I do not think you can have received my letter," she went on flatly, "nor the letter written to you by my uncle, Mr. John Honeyman, who is an attorney in London, or you would have known that we proposed coming to live with you—my brother, my sister and myself."

"I did receive some letters a while since." His face changed suddenly and he seemed at a loss: he was more than a little drunk. "I put 'em on the fire."

"Without reading them, I presume, otherwise you would know that my father—your son—is dead." She waited, but if she had hoped for some expression of remorse or sorrow she was disappointed.

"I read as far as that and it was enough," he said surlily, slurring his words. "And if you think you are going to be given house-room here you are mistaken." At that the woman behind her uttered a shrill laugh and Martha waited until she was quiet before she said firmly and clearly:

"I beg your pardon, sir, but it is you who are mistaken. I would not dream of allowing my sister or my brother to take up residence under this roof. Your house is not fit for a pig to live in—let alone the children of a gentleman." She picked up her skirts, turned her back on him and his woman and whirled out of the room.

"Stop, you termagant!" shouted Henry Lingford after her. "Where are you going?"

"Back to Rydd of course." She threw the reply over her shoulder at him. "I shall engage rooms at the George for tonight and tomorrow we shall leave the town. You will not be troubled with us again. Good night, sir."

Before the servant could get to the front door she was there and had slammed it behind her and was running up the path back to the carriage.

"It is not possible to stay there," she told the two young people who were waiting for her there goggle-eyed, and she ignored the grinning coachman. "Get back into the carriage, my dears. We must stay a night in Rydd and then tomorrow we will return to London."

"But where are we to go in London?" asked Sukey as the carriage door closed behind them and they started back to Rydd. "To my uncle's?"

"Possibly for a time," agreed Martha. She did not see what else she could do.

By the time the morning came, however, she had changed her mind, and directly they had breakfasted she told her brother and sister to accompany her into the town as she wanted to look for lodgings.

"Lodgings in Rydd?" Sukey was dismayed. She had not been at all averse to returning to London and exploring some of its wonderful warehouses. "But my uncle said—"

"I know what he said, my love, and I have no doubt

that he meant it. But until it becomes a case of dire necessity—as it may well do—we cannot impose on him or on my aunt. So I have decided to take lodgings in Rydd, saving the expense of another journey, and London lodgings which would be far more expensive, until we have heard from the lords of the Admiralty about their Royal Naval School in Portsmouth. I intend to write to them tomorrow, enclosing Admiral Wintersham's letter, but first of all we must find an address to which they can reply."

"But—should not my grandfather write?" Charles tried to hide his dismay that his future should be decided for him by a woman, even if she did happen to be his sister. He had had enough of petticoat government and had been looking forward to meeting his grandfather: it now seemed he was not to be allowed to do that.

"I shall not ask him to write, Charles." From what Martha had seen of Mr. Lingford the night before she thought it highly improbable that he would ever be in a fit state to hold a pen. If he were to receive a reply from their lordships, moreover, it was extremely likely that he would follow his usual custom of throwing it on the fire unread. "No, Charles. You must trust this to me. Your future depends on it and we cannot risk such an important prospect in considering the whims of a . . ." She was about to say "drunken" and changed it quickly to "senile old man."

They searched the whole morning without finding suitable lodgings, those near the harbour being noisy and dirty, and others in better quarters being too small or too high in price. And then at about two o'clock they came upon the Bowery, a cottage belonging to a fisherman's widow and situated on the coast road beyond a boat-builder's yard. It was a neat little house, its windows shone, its shutters were newly painted, and the little garden in front was well kept, while at the rear a vegetable patch had rows of peas already up and gooseberry bushes beside an old apple tree. A pear tree was growing against the cottage wall and Mrs. Spry pointed it out to them with pride.

"Sir William Connington give me that," she told them. She was a nice little woman, neat and clean in her person and anxious to please. "It was the year my husband was lost, poor dear. Sir William comes to see me and her ladyship with him. 'Lucy,' she says—I was a maid once at Meldrum many years ago—'Lucy, we are getting up a fund for you, and Sir William reckons it will be enough for you to live on in this cottage so that you'll always have a roof over your head,' she says. 'And to show that he means what he says we've brought you a pear tree to plant alongside your cottage wall.' And though they say he who plants pears plants for his heirs, it's given me more than a few juicy ones this last year or more."

Martha had only to glance at the rooms to pronounce herself to be satisfied.

There was a small bedroom above the porch for Charles, a large one for herself and Sukey, and a small dressing-room opening off it for Betsy. The beds had dimity counterpanes and white curtains billowed out in the salty air that came in at the windows, while downstairs a roomy, low-pitched parlour awaited them for meals and for pleasure.

Moreover in the small garden looking across the bay pinks and thrift and lavender grew together happily with marjoram and thyme, reminding her of their old home in Crome.

She arranged with Mrs. Spry that they would move in that afternoon and they went back to the George Inn to pack, to eat their dinner and to settle their account before engaging the coach again to take them to the Bowery.

"It is the last day of April," Martha noted in the pocket book that Charles had given her. "Tomorrow is the first of May."

There was something very encouraging in the thought that summer was on its way.

Four

To Betsy's simple mind the quality always had money to spare. It was only the poor, like herself, who lived from hand to mouth.

And Miss Lingford, she told Mrs. Spry over a cosy chat in the latter's kitchen on the night after they arrived at the Bowery, was that book-learned. She kept her father's housekeeping books for him from the time she was twelve, the poor gentleman being distracted after his wife's death.

On the first morning Martha brought out the pocket book again and entered in it all that she had spent since their father died. She had sent Charles and Sukey out for a walk along the shore so that she could study such things in peace before starting on the all-important letter to their lordships at the Admiralty.

Betsy's wages of five pounds had been paid for the year at Christmas, and the money that their uncle had given them had paid for their journey from London to Rydd, there being sufficient out of it to pay the two shillings for the chaise to the Bowery.

She reckoned that ten pounds a month would pay for their lodgings and their keep, which meant that one hundred pounds should last them for ten months. A second hundred must be kept at all costs for Charles. Sir Thomas had told her when he gave her the letter that it would cost "merely sixty or seventy pounds" to start him off in Portsmouth. If they moved to cheaper lodgings in Portsmouth she felt she might be able to obtain employment herself in teaching music. She played the pianoforte well enough to teach, if she could cultivate the necessary patience for it—never a strong point with her.

From where she sat she could see her brother and sister clearly. The masts of the boats were like a forest rising from the harbour beyond and the sun danced on the water and the boats, while Sukey searched for shells in the shingle and Charles sat himself down on an upturned rowing boat and began an earnest conversation with one of the fishermen there.

Martha watched him smiling. He loved the sea and he should have his chance: she would fight for that whatever it cost.

She put her pocket book away and started to write her letter, but it was hard to know how to put what she had to say to their lordships, and as she hunted for words, she saw a cart making its way along the coast road from the town towards the boat-yard and the Bowery. The cart was driven by an old gentleman and she did not recognize him until he stopped outside the cottage, threw the reins to the servant beside him, and got down stiffly to come stomping up the path to knock on Mrs. Spry's door.

Martha waited apprehensively while her landlady went to open it, wondering if she would detect outrage in Mrs. Spry's voice when she recognized her visitor, but she sounded not only friendly but welcoming as she said, "Why, Mr. Lingford, sir, it is a long while since I see you. I hope as your gout is better, sir?"

"Thank 'ee, ma'am. It don't trouble me much this fine weather. I understand you have some young relatives of mine staying here. Be so good as to take me to them."

"Miss Lingford is in the parlour, sir. Will you please to step in?" The parlour door opened and Martha rose to meet her grandfather, flushing with surprise and annoyance. Had she not shown him plainly that she wished to have no more to do with him?

He certainly looked cleaner this morning: his grey worsted stockings had no holes in them, his black shoes had steel buckles that might have shone like silver had anyone taken the trouble to polish them, and his black breeches were buttoned with steel buttons at the knee. His brown coat was shabby but his shirt was clean— or at least the neckerchief above it was clean. He had been shaved this morning, while under his round hat his white hair was brushed and tied back neatly.

But it was at his face that she looked and she was pleased to see that his eyes could not meet hers.

"I have come to apologize for the night you came to see me," he said gruffly. "I had no right to speak as

I did, even if I was drunk at the time. I suppose my son left you all penniless?"

"Certainly not." Three hundred pounds was not penury.

"And your mother? Is she alive?"

"She died about ten years ago."

"That's a blessing." He held up his hand. "No need to flash your eyes at me like that. I meant nothing. What made you take these lodgings? To embarrass me, I suppose?"

"I did not think of you when I took them." Her eyes met his with angry contempt. "It was entirely to suit my own convenience. I cannot afford to make fruitless journeys about the country and there is my brother's future to be considered. When you walked in I was composing a letter to the lords of the Admiralty to ask them to enter Charles in their school in Portsmouth in July, when he will be fourteen years of age."

"And may I ask what you know about such things?"

"Only what a friend of my Uncle Josiah Honeyman's in Bath—Admiral Sir Thomas Wintersham—told me, and what he advised me to do. He gave me a letter to the Admiralty enclosed in one to you, but I did not think it worth while to trouble you with it, knowing that it would find its way to the fire unread, and Charles's future is too important to me for that. I intend to enclose Sir Thomas's letter in one of mine, as it appears to be a warm recommendation. He thinks Charles is the type of lad that the Admiralty needs to train for its officers."

"Does he indeed? I am greatly obliged to him. And what excuse will you offer for writing to their lordships? I presume you realize that such a letter would come better from Charles's grandfather than from yourself?"

"Of course I realize it, But if you were to write and the reply came to you neither Charles nor I would know anything about it. My excuse therefore will be that you are too indisposed these days to write letters."

"The devil it will." He glared at her. "I called you a termagant, and by God you are one. Give me those letters."

She gave them to him reluctantly, half expecting him to tear them up, but instead he read the letter to himself carefully before perusing the one that had been enclosed in it. He was silent for a moment, scowling at the floor, and then he said abruptly, "Sit down at that table and take up your pen and a fresh sheet of paper."

"I beg your pardon?" She did not quite know how to proceed so unexpected was the request.

"Do as I say, girl. Take your pen and write."

She sat down and drawing a sheet of paper towards her she dipped her pen in the inkwell and waited. He walked to the window and with his eyes on the sea he dictated a letter that surprised her in its direct approach to the matter in hand.

My Lords,
While aware that my grandson is approaching four-teen and that your lordships prefer boys to enter your school in Portsmouth at the age of eleven or twelve, I am told by Admiral Sir Thomas Wintersham that in the case of a promising lad you might waive that rule and give him the requisite schooling before sending him to sea. I enclose a letter from Admiral Sir Thomas Wintersham who has met the boy and is kind enough to add his recommendation to mine. Your lordships' obedient servant

He had got thus far when the door burst open and Charles came in.

"Martha!" he cried excitedly. "There is an old fisherman on the beach by the boat-yard and he says he will take me out in his boat and teach me to sail. When he heard my name he said, 'There never was a Lingford yet that couldn't handle a boat.' What do you think of that?" He stopped short. "I beg your pardon. I did not see that there was anyone with you."

"Your grandfather, Charles," Martha said unsmiling, as she finished the letter and waited while Henry Lingford signed it.

"My grandfather?" Charles advanced eagerly and as the old gentleman threw down the pen he held out his hand. "I am very glad to meet you, sir. I have heard much about you from my father."

"Nothing to my advantage, I'll be bound." But the old man put out his hand in spite of himself to grip the youngster's.

"Oh no, sir. That is to say, yes sir. My father always said what a spanking good driver you were. A four-in-hand, he said was nothing to you. I was hoping you would be able to teach me: I've two great ambitions, do you see, sir. One is to be an officer in the Royal Navy and the second is to drive a four-in-hand." He paused, suddenly embarrassed. "But of course, sir, that was before we discovered that you had lost your money."

"Lost my money? What on earth is the boy talking about?" Henry Lingford glared at Martha. "What is this story you have been putting about?"

"I think, sir, that Charles is only going by appearances." Martha's voice was coldly controlled. "When he saw your house two nights ago—even in the twilight —he could see at once that it was not the house of a rich man. And then we heard in the town that you had sold Emmetts many years ago. I believe it is usual for gentlemen to sell their estates if they wish to face their creditors."

"You speak your mind, madam, damned if you don't." He seemed about to explode with wrath and then his eyes went past her to the window. "Who the hell is that?" he demanded.

Martha turned her head. "That is my sister, Sukey," she said, satisfied that her sister's looks had not failed to impress her grandfather: it was the natural reaction of any man, young or old, when he first saw Sukey. The girl came in and she introduced her to her grandfather and Sukey smiled radiantly, came to him and kissed him.

"I hope you are well, Grandfather?" she said.

"Quite well, thank you, my dear." He could not take his eyes off her. Why, he thought, the girl was a raving beauty. Did that sour sister of hers not realize what she had on her hands? If she were to be introduced into the fashionable world she would have every man after her, and if he were not so old he would take her into that world himself. But he had stepped out of it many years ago.

He jammed his hat on his head and said he must be going, and then as he reached the door he came back and taking a purse from his coat pocket he threw it on the table in front of Martha.

"Fifty guineas," he said. "To pay for your lodgings. Good day to you." And the next moment he was out of the house and making his way to the gate where his little cart was waiting.

"I think you are mistaken in our grandfather, Martha," Charles said, highly gratified. "He is a kind old fellow."

"He is *sweet*!" said Sukey.

Martha folded Admiral Sir Thomas Wintersham's letter into the one she had written for her grandfather and hoped that their lordships would not object to paying for a double letter.

"I wish I had shown him some of my things," Charles said. "But I have not unpacked them yet. And I want to tell you about that old fisherman, Martha."

He told her about the fisherman, while Sukey arranged a handful of coloured shells along the chimney-piece and said what a pretty necklace they would make.

Martha listened to them with an indulgent smile and then she took the purse of guineas upstairs and locked it away in her small trunk with the money that constituted their worldly wealth. She detested her grandfather as much if not more, than she had done on the night that she met him in his dirty old house with that slut beside him to keep him company. But she was bound to admit that he might be better off than she had thought.

And then they all walked to the town to post the letter to their lordships before they had their dinner.

Old Henry Lingford drove back in silence through the town and out of the west gate and as he came on to the marsh and passed the belt of trees with Rydd House standing up bare and bleak from the road, for the first time he saw it through other eyes than his own.

The lichened piers, the padlocked gates—one adrift from a broken hinge—the stone pineapple lying among the nettles, the grass waist-high in the courtyard, and the house beyond with its shuttered windows and loose slates that had never been replaced, all gave the impression of poverty and decay. What had that young termagant said about it? Something about it not being fit for a pig to live in, "let alone the children of a gentleman".

As he ate the dinner that the old crone who passed for a cook in his kitchen served up to him he turned many things over in his mind. The meal seemed more unappetizing than usual that day and his eyes left his plate to travel round the dark dining-parlour and compare it with the brightness of the little room in the Bowery, with Charles's eager young face and Sukey's loveliness to brighten it still more.

Of Martha he thought as little as he could, because every time she looked at him it had been from Vincent's eyes. The shape of her face, the lift of her head, the way she held herself, were all Vincent: his son would never be dead while she lived, and neither, God help him, would his conscience.

After the meal was done and his manservant, Ben Heavers, had cleared the dishes, he sent for his groom, Jonas Pegg, who was also employed in growing vegetables when he was not looking after the ponies, Fidget and Placid, and cleaning the stables, and he told him to get his scythe and start mowing the grass in front of the house.

"But—" The man stared. "It's not been done in years, sir."

"All the more reason to do it now." The old man jammed on his hat again and walked to the town and climbed a narrow passage to North Street and visited the forge there, and saw the blacksmith, Goliath Pipe. There were many occasions when he went to see Mr. Pipe, not connected with a blacksmith's work, but this time it was different.

" 'Afternoon, Pipe," he said. "Want those gates of mine repaired and re-hung. Hinge on one of 'em is broken."

"It's been broken this last ten years or more, Mr. Lingford, sir," said Goliath, staring as Jonas had stared.

"See to it then. I need a new lock too, so that the padlock can be removed. Get a locksmith to it. Those gates have to be made to open again."

"Very well, sir. I will see to it for you."

"Mind you do. And I need a plasterer and stone-mason to repair the pineapple that's fallen, and a painter to give the gates a coat of paint. Jonathan Whip is the best stonemason in the town. Bring him with you tomorrow."

"It will cost you a penny or two, Mr. Lingford, sir," said Goliath and the old man flushed angrily. So the whole town thought he was penniless did they?

"As the pennies will be mine and not yours it's my business alone," he snapped, and went back to his house in an angry mood.

"Seems like the old gentleman is breaking up," Goliath told his friend Jonathan Whip in the Mariners' Arms down by the harbour that night. "Unlike him to spend money on the place."

The following morning when the two of them went to shake their heads over the gates and the stone pineapple at Rydd House they heard from Jonas, busy scything the grass in the courtyard, that the old man had dismissed his doxy the night before. "Sent her off at a moment's notice," he told them with a grin. "And when she turned saucy he said he'd take his whip to her if she didn't take and goo. Reckon he would, too."

Jonathan said the old gentleman must be going senile.

They were more sure of it still when a glazier appeared to replace broken windows, and another man came to replace tiles on the roof, while Willy Fortune the sweep arrived to sweep the chimneys, bringing his son with him.

Nothing had been done to the house, not a farthing spent on it, since Henry Lingford had moved there over ten years ago. Before that he had let it to a farmer who neglected it for more profitable activities on the marsh, and he had let it go to rack and ruin for years.

Mr. Lingford had moved into it as it was and not a finger had been lifted to put it in repair until today. He was going senile, they said, or else he had lost his wits completely.

Five

While these things were going on at Rydd House its owner took his morning walk by way of a track across the marsh to the shore and thence to the harbour and the boat-yard where he would stay to talk to the men who worked there. The Bowery was only a step from the boat-yard but he did not call there until one morning just as he was leaving the yard he saw his grandson in the cottage porch busy cleaning something that caught the May sunshine.

There was no sign of his sisters and curiosity got the better of the old gentleman. He walked the fifty yards or so to the Bowery and leaned his arms on the little gate with his eyes on Charles and his most prized possessions.

"Good morning, Charles," he said. "What have you got there?"

"Oh, good morning, Grandfather." Charles looked up, pleased at seeing him there. "These are some pistols I'm cleaning. The girls are out in the town buying satin for Sukey's slippers. Come and look at these—aren't they beauties?"

Henry Lingford pushed back the little gate and walked up the path with alacrity: he would not admit how eagerly he seized this opportunity to speak to his grandson again.

The pistols were in a wooden box, finely worked in marquetry, as the steel of the pistol boxes was worked in the finest and most intricate patterns. "Duelling pistols!" he said, surprised. "Where did you get them, boy?"

"They were left to my father by a friend who was killed at the battle of Bunker's Hill in America. They were specially made for him. Are they not beautiful, sir?"

"They are very fine weapons indeed." Henry Lingford lifted the pistols carefully out of their case, handling them tenderly and examining the worked barrels, the finely wrought steel of the butts, and the crest of the man who had left them to his dead son—a hawk with a mouse in its beak. "They are not too heavy to handle either," he went on as he took them up and tried them. "They fit into the hand as a nicely balanced weapon should." He raised one and squinted along its barrel. "Can you fire them, boy?"

"No, sir, I've never tried." Charles added wistfully, "I would like to practice on the marshes here early in the morning when nobody is about, but I fancy my powder is damp."

"It is no use to fire with damp powder: pistols like

these could blow up in your face." The old man pondered a moment, his eyes fixed thoughtfully on the boy. "And I would not be too sure either that the marshes *are* empty in the early morning. But if you will bring them to my house tomorrow at ten o'clock we will take them out together and I will show you how to load and to fire. I know many empty stretches where we shall do no damage to humans or to sheep. What do you say to that, young Charles?"

Charles was in ecstasies. He told Martha about his grandfather's offer when the girls got back and at first he was afraid by the expression on his elder sister's face that she might be going to oppose it. But she agreed reluctantly that it would be a useful occupation for her brother, and that no doubt he would have to learn to fire such weapons when he was an officer in the Royal Navy.

She watched him go on the following day with misgivings. She was deeply suspicious of old Henry Lingford and she wondered what was at the back of his offer. She was almost convinced that he would never do anything for his grandchildren unless there was a motive behind it.

For the next week or more Charles visited his grandfather every morning, and the weather remaining fine and dry they made their way to a lonely part of the marsh where it ran down to the sea. With the sheep too far distant to lend themselves as targets Henry Lingford taught his grandson how to load, to prime, to ram the powder down and to fire. He found the boy an apt pupil, and his wrists were already strong enough to bring the weapons up steadily to fire. His aim might be deplorable but with so great a will to improve his tutor did not despair of making a first class shot of him in the finish.

The men working in the boat-builder's yard grew accustomed to seeing them walking back together to the Bowery, the old man with his long white hair blowing in the wind and the boy's fair hair as short as his sisters' fringes.

By the end of a fortnight Henry Lingford told Charles that his aim was improving. "I believe you might be able to hit a haystack now at a range of five yards," he added chuckling, as one sunny morning they ended their practice. "I would like to see you aim at one of those sheep yonder, but I do not wish to be hauled up before the Bench. The justices round about are not too fond of me as 'tis."

"Why?" Charles was surprised.

"There are certain transactions I indulge in that do not meet with their approval," Henry Lingford said dryly and would say no more.

Martha's misgivings were lulled for a time by Charles's evident enjoyment of his mornings, and she was interested to learn that Rydd House was undergoing repairs. Charles told her about it after he had walked back to the Bowery that morning with his grandfather. The old man never came in: he would turn about quickly and start walking back at once, leaving Charles to run up the path and enter the cottage alone.

"And what is more," added Charles triumphantly, "I think he has given that woman her marching orders."

"What woman?" Martha had forgotten that her brother and sister had been interested witnesses of her reception at Rydd House.

"Why, the woman who was there on that first

evening when we arrived from London," Charles said.

"I didn't realize that you could see her from the road," Martha said.

"She was so painted up that her face shone out like a sunset," said Charles. "We saw her again today. She was waiting outside the gate as we left the house, pinked more than ever, and finely dressed with coque-licot ribbons all over her, and she said something to Grandfather and bobbed a curtsey, smiling and ogling him—and me too, for that matter! But Grandfather was equal to her. He sent her off pretty smartish and told her that if he found her round the place again the dogs would be at her." Charles laughed. "He's got two dogs he uses for coursing hares, and if they went after her as fiercely as they go after hares I'm sorry for her. I suppose she was his doxy wasn't she, Martha?"

"That is a word that is not used in polite society," said his sister severely.

"I beg your pardon." He was silent, momentarily abashed, and then he said with an irrepressible burst of laughter, "But I should not think my grandfather's society was ever polite!" And then Sukey came down-stairs to join them in her new satin slippers and he produced some fine coloured shells from his pockets for her necklace.

Mr. Lingford's behaviour continued to puzzle his elder grand-daughter. She wondered if he were planning to invite them to live at Rydd House, and if he did so she did not know what she should do. She was quite sure it would not be nearly as snug and comfortable as the dear little Bowery, and she had no wish to place her brother and sister and herself under the roof and the rule of such an old renegade. As long as she could she would cling to her independence. She asked Charles if there were many servants at the house.

"There's an old woman in the kitchen," he told her. "I would not like to eat anything she prepares though. She takes snuff all the time and drops it into everything, while from the smell of spirits in the kitchen I would say she indulges in Geneva pretty frequently too."

"Are there no others?" Martha was half horrified, half fascinated.

"No more maidservants."

"And menservants?"

"Two. His groom Jonas Pegg, who acts as gardener too, and his personal servant Ben Heavers, who waits on him at table and makes the fires in the rooms and fetches the newspapers from Rydd, and I expect he fetches the letters too if there are any, but I daresay all Grandfather's friends gave up writing to him years ago."

"And who sweeps and dusts the place?" asked Sukey.

"Ben, if he thinks of it." Charles laughed at the expression on his sisters' faces. "The dust is so thick in the dining-parlour that you could write your name a dozen times on the table. But I daresay it is difficult to persuade maidservants to go there with—" He suddenly halted, remembering what Martha had said on the subject, and added lamely: "the sort of company he keeps. Once a house has a name for—that sort of thing, you know—girls might not like to take a situation there."

"What sort of company?" asked Sukey innocently. "Martha dear, what *is* Charles talking about?"

"Only Charles knows." Martha frowned at her

brother. "And here is Betsy with our dinner—soles caught in the bay this morning and fried as only Mrs. Spry can fry them, and don't they smell good?"

The ditches and dykes of the marsh were separated from the shore by a natural steep bank of shingle. Once, many years ago, the townsmen of Rydd had been taken with the idea that it would be an excellent thing if they were to clear the shingle, and wagons and oxen had been set to work to take it away and to level the shore to the marsh, but in a very little while the storms and the tides and the waves rolling in had brought it all back and piled it up on a bank every bit as strong and invincible as the first.

There were some no doubt who did not regret it, as the bank made a convenient shelter when boats were brought in to be unloaded by moonshine. One morning after a practice that had been shorter than usual because of the uncompromising weather—the wide expanse of sky had suddenly discovered a cluster of black clouds in the west and was sending them scurrying towards Rydd—Charles and his grandfather made for the far side of the shingle bank, instead of walking along the top of it to the town. The wind that was blowing off the land was cold enough for snow and threatened to blight every bud on the fruit trees in and around Rydd.

"We'll walk along the shore beyond the bank," Mr. Lingford said. "This wind is finding out my old bones."

The high bank shut them in with its protection: the sun came out, the black clouds altered course and headed for France, and the beach was as empty as ever. Sandpipers were busy at the water's edge and some gulls were looking for worms in a stretch of sand that appeared at low tide and as they came in sight of the harbour Charles saw something lying against a clump of reeds. It looked like a bundle of old clothes or a drift of seaweed left by the receding tide. He ran to see what it was and then shouted to his grandfather, white-faced.

"Grandfather! There's a man lying down here and I think he's been drowned. Come quickly."

"If he has been drowned," said his grandfather coolly, "there is no sense in hurrying." But he joined his grandson where the body was lying, washed up under the reeds. It had been in the water for a few days and the tattered clothing left little by which it could be identified. As it lay there huddled against the reeds, as cold as the water that oozed from its garments old Lingford studied it frowning.

"Breeches pockets turned out and empty," he said, "No jewellery. Look inside his shirt, boy, and see if you can find anything sewn into it." Then, seeing him hesitate, "Quick, lad. You will see more dead bodies than one if you are going into the Royal Navy."

Charles opened the front of the shirt distastefully and found nothing under the stained remains of what had once been a lace jabot, and his grandfather told him to look at the inside of the breeches. "There may be something in the waist that they've overlooked," he said.

This second search was more rewarding. Under the fastening Charles found a small flat leather packet, so small as to be easily mistaken for a repair to the fastening itself. Charles cut it adrift with his pocket knife and handed it to his grandfather in silence.

Inside the packet there was a scrap of paper with pointed handwriting on it and a seal, and after a glance at it the old man nodded and said tersely, "Thought so. A Frenchie."

"French?" Charles got to his feet staring at the remains in the reeds. "An *émigré*, do you mean, sir?"

"What else? The poor wretch no doubt started rowing for England, and not being accustomed to oars, gave up in mid-Channel, where some of our fishermen hailed him and offered assistance. They then persuaded him to transfer his valuables to their boat, cut his throat and tipped him overboard. At least that is my reading of the matter. It has happened before."

"Cut his throat?" Charles stared at the Frenchman's body and in particular at a brown gash where the throat had been. But surely Englishmen would not have done a thing like this to a fugitive seeking safety from the guillotine? Sickened, he thought of the kindly fishermen and boat-builders he had made his friends since he had been in Rydd. He could not believe that any of them would have been a party to such a treacherous act.

"Men will do a great deal for money," his grandfather said grimly, as if he read his thoughts. He looked at the scrap of paper and the seal. "Can you read French, lad?"

"Afraid I can't, sir."

"Pity. No more can I. But that lace was Mechlin, or I'm a Dutchman, and this seal is the signature of somebody important. I think we must ask Sir William Connington to come and look at him. He may be that friend of his who was expected in Rydd last Wednesday night. The boat that was sent for him missed him in the fog that came down out in the Channel. In the meantime we cannot leave him here." He looked at the tide that had reached its ebb and would soon be on the turn. "The harbour will be idle for the next hour or so. Run to the boat-yard and tell James Crew and Matthew Ribston to come here at once and to bring with them a piece of old sailcloth or something of the sort to carry him in."

"The Bowery is not much further," Charles said. "Could I not fetch a blanket from there?"

"We do not want to spoil a good blanket with a corpse," said Henry Lingford. "And we do not want a pack of chattering women about us. Run, boy! Do as I say and do not waste time."

Charles ran off along a quayside that was without its usual activity. Boats were lying on their sides in the mud, and a few fishermen were sitting on the quay mending nets, but they scarcely looked up as Charles went by. In a very few minutes he returned with the men his grandfather had asked for and one other, Sam Last by name, who had just returned from the chandler's shop. They did not seem to think the finding of a corpse on the shore to be anything unusual and they lifted the remains of the Frenchman into the piece of sailcloth they had brought with a lack of concern that struck the boy as being singularly cold-blooded. But after all, he thought, as he watched them, why should Englishmen be concerned over one more dead Frenchman? Were we not at war with France?

"Now take him back to the shed," ordered Mr. Lingford, his voice carrying authority, and they carried him back and laid their burden down on a pile of wood shavings in a corner.

"He can be left there for the present," Mr. Lingford went on. "You, James and Matthew, and you, Sam Last, with my grandson here, are to keep an eye on the corpse until I return. Do not allow anybody to remove it from here. I am setting out at once on one of the George chaises for Meldrum and I intend to bring back Sir William Connington with me."

He hurried away across the quay in the direction of the steep little street that led to the town square while the three men looked to Charles for an explanation. Was the corpse known to Mr. Lingford, they wanted to know? He shook his head.

"I don't think so." He did not quite know how much he should tell them. "Perhaps my grandfather thinks he should fetch Sir William Connington because he is a justice of the peace, you know."

"Aye," said James, with a glance at the other two. "He is a justice of the peace, as some of us know to our cost."

They cast uneasy glances at the stiff figure under the sailcloth in the shavings. "There's many drowned round the coast hereabouts from time to time," said Sam Last then, slowly. "Why make such a pother of this 'un?"

"I think," Charles said, still choosing his words, "it may be because he was not drowned."

"Not drownded?" They stared at him, but he had the feeling that they had guessed it for themselves.

"My grandfather said that his throat had been cut," he said, and again he had the feeling that this came as no surprise to them either, but only Sam Last ventured to come across to the corner to lift the sailcloth and stare for a moment at what lay there before covering it again and returning to his work without a word.

Charles sat down in the shavings, with a straw in his mouth, chewing it thoughtfully, the case with his pistols beside him.

Somehow the boatshed had lost its magic: the three men from being friends, ready to answer questions and to explain what they were doing and why, had become suddenly remote. They ignored him and talked together in low tones so that he could not hear what they were saying.

The clouds had blown up again and the salt air, usually so fresh and clean, turned cold, while the smell of freshly sawn wood and tar was overpowered by the poor thing beside him in the corner. Even the swallows, swooping in and out from their nests in the rafters, were distantly unfriendly.

But he sat on there stolidly, because he thought the three men would have been glad to see him gone, chewing his straw and throwing stones from time to time at the rats that scampered about the shed.

When Betsy arrived in a fury at three o'clock to tell him that dinner was on the table and to ask why he had not come home for it he did not budge.

"I thought I'd find you here in this old shed," she said wrathfully. "You come along of me at once."

"I will come when my grandfather returns," he said.

"He don't trust us, missus," said Sam with a laugh, and James Crew added bitterly that maybe he thought the corpse in the corner would get up and walk away.

"Corpse?" Betsy stared at the sailcloth and her red face lost some of its colour.

"Don't take on, Betsy," Charles said. "We found a dead man lying on the shore and my grandfather has gone to fetch Sir William Connington—the justice of the peace, you know—and he told me to wait here until he returns. It was striking twelve on the town clock soon after he left so that he should be back soon. Keep my dinner hot for me, Betsy, there's a dear, and take my case of pistols back to the Bowery with you."

"They ain't loaded, Master Charles?" Betsy looked at the case with almost as much horror as she had looked at the sailcloth.

"No, of course not, Betsy." He gave the case to her. "But be very careful not to drop it."

She said she would be very careful, and went away and finding an impatient Martha waiting for her brother's return at the Bowery, she poured out the story of the drowned man. "It's put me all of a tremble," she told her young mistress. "And then these here Things of Master Charles's. He said I was not to drop 'em, even though they ain't loaded."

"Give them to me, Betsy." Martha was as usual firmly in control of the situation. "And then come and sit down and take some wine to restore you. When we have had our dinner I shall go to the boat-yard and take Charles's place there."

"That ain't woman's work, my dear!" protested Betsy, while Sukey gave a small shriek of horror.

"Among those rough men, too!" she said. "It's not the thing for a lady to do, Martha!"

"If there is such work to be done then it should be done, by a man or a woman, and being a lady has nothing to do with it," said Martha. "Come now, Betsy, drink the wine, and then we will have our dinner."

Six

Mr. Connington spent three weeks in Gloucestershire and the enthusiasm he had felt for his charming little manor house faded with his enthusiasm for his sheep. It amused him to play the farmer, but for other entertainment there were occasional concerts or a play at the theatre in the little town of Ainswick five miles off, or the society of a neighbouring squire, the owner of five hundred acres and four plain daughters. He could find no joy in such company and fled to Kent.

His mother was delighted to see him. "And how is Arcott?" she asked fondly, watching him eat his breakfast in the library on the morning after his arrival while his father, with whom she had breakfasted some hours previously, was occupied in the justice room.

"A great bore," he said smiling.

"That is because you breed sheep. They are most unintelligent animals. Farming should be left to farmers, Drum." And then as he did not reply, "You need a wife, dear."

"I do not need a wife, Mamma. A mistress is equally satisfying—for a time."

His mother poured out his coffee and said coolly: "I conclude that Lady Duffington is still your companion?"

"You are mistaken. I found a letter waiting at Arcott to tell me that she married Patrick O'Malley the week I left London."

"My poor Drum. How mean of Lord O'Malley!"

"Not at all. I am eternally grateful to him. Anna Duffington is beautiful but her head is as empty as a blown egg."

Lady Connington regarded him hopelessly. "I still say that you need a wife," she said. "Did your sister not introduce you to any nice young ladies in Bath?"

"Several dozen or so, all very accomplished and flatteringly anxious to become Mrs. Drum Connington."

"In one of her letters Fanny said there were two nice girls living in Bath with their parents—Honeyman, I think was the name. Did you meet them?"

"I did. Fine fillies both, with more stamina than breeding. Either of them would have made me a good wife and bred strong children—and I should have murdered her in a fortnight."

"You are hard to please. But now that you are in Kent again will you not consider Leonora Racksby? I have always thought that she would suit you admirably."

"Now what makes you think that?"

"She is vivacious, witty and a good conversationalist, she is handsome, an excellent horsewoman, and very accomplished."

"I detest witty women who make conversation."

"Surely you would hate them still more if they sat dumb all the evening?"

"I would prefer them to keep quiet if they have nothing to say. The witty Leonora says so much about so little."

She changed the subject and asked him if he approved of the horses his father had found for his inspection.

"I am to try them in the shafts this morning, and as long as they do not kick my new carriage to bits I am very much obliged to my father. The horse-breeders round Ainswick are rogues."

She came to the conclusion that he was tired after his journey, or else that he was more wounded by Lady Duffington's desertion than he would admit. Persevering in her efforts to talk him into a better temper she once more changed the subject to a topic that she fancied might be more acceptable.

"Did your father tell you that Harry Redfern is back in Rydd?"

"He did not." The frown left his face. "What is he doing there?"

"Why, he has been made captain of the Rydd Excise cutter, the *Snipe* I think it is called. Everyone is so pleased, and of course Mr. and Mrs. Redfern are delighted to have him there."

"Naturally." Some of the languor that Drum Connington deliberately cultivated left him as he thought of his old school-friend.

When he was seven years old his father had removed him from the entirely feminine company of his six sisters and their governess and placed him in Mr. Bridges's school in Rydd as a parlour boarder.

Some years previously the Reverend Nathaniel Bridges had been appointed as curate to the parish of St. Peter's in Rydd, and found himself burdened with a large house, a family that increased with unfailing regularity every year, and a salary of thirty-six pounds a year on which to keep them. As he was a good Greek scholar and an excellent mathematician, he started a school for the sons of gentlemen and advertised for boarders, which was a boon for the country gentlemen outside the town, whose large houses were apt to be marooned in chalky mud during the winter months. Moreover, so excellent was Mr. Bridges' tuition and so kindly his disposition, and so motherly his wife in looking after the boys' health, that by the time Drum joined the school Mr. Bridges was already employing two ushers.

Drum settled down happily and made a friend there in the younger son of a maltster who at that time was mayor of Rydd—a boy of his own age by the name of Harry Redfern. So close in fact did their friendship become that having met the first day behind the garden shed to black each other's eyes and bloody each other's nose, they were that inseparable, only parting when Drum left the school for Winchester and Harry was transferred to the Rydd Grammar School. But their friendship remained close and during the long summer holidays the two boys would spend weeks together, Harry at Meldrum and Drum in Rydd, and they would swim and fish and ride and course hares and help to drain the Meldrum fishponds and catch the eels there, and set their terriers on the rats in the rickyards, with all the joy that such activities inspired in schoolboys.

It was only later after Drum went up to Oxford and then abroad for a year with a tutor on the Grand Tour of European capitals, while Harry joined the Navy, transferring from it later to Customs and Excise, that they lost sight of each other.

Now, however, there was every prospect that they would meet again and it was with a feeling of pleasure in that prospect that Drum went off to try out his new horses.

He came back at half past one in time to see a chaise crossing the park in a hurry, and he asked his mother if she was expecting anybody to visit her.

She left her embroidery to join him in the parlour window. "It looks like old Mr. Lingford," she said, as the chaise stopped and an old gentleman was helped out by the post-boy. "Yes, I am sure it is he. I wonder if he has news of M. de Salle."

"Why should Mr. Lingford have news of him?"

"Because the marquis wrote to your father some weeks ago telling him that he had arrived on the coast near Boulogne with his wife, his younger son and his married daughter and her child. His eldest son and his daughter's husband had been murdered by the revolutionaries. He was to leave his family with a trusted servant while he came across to England to make arrangements for their reception and he asked your father to send a fishing boat or some such vessel to find him in mid-Channel and bring him the rest of the way to Rydd. They arranged some sort of signal so that the captain of the boat should recognize him.

At all events your father went to see Mr. Lingford, knowing that he has the best knowledge of the fishermen in Rydd."

"I should say there is scarcely a fisherman—or smuggler—that is not known to the old rascal, would not you?"

She smiled. "He certainly very soon found one to meet M. de Salle's requirements—the *Turk*, a large fishing boat with a cabin below."

"And when is this boat to set out?" asked her son and she was pleased to see animation in his face.

"It set out last Wednesday night, and when M. de Salle did not arrive Mr. Lingford made enquiries from the captain of the *Turk*, thinking that he had not gone, and he was told that a fog had come down in the Channel and he had been unable to find M. de Salle or to see any signals at all. Of course M. de Salle may have been apprehended at Boulogne and taken back to Paris with his family, and if that has happened I shall be very sorry for the poor creatures but a little relieved on my own account. I am not anxious to entertain French *émigrés* for any length of time at Meldrum."

"Do not be so uncharitable, Mamma."

"Indeed I am not being uncharitable, Drum. I am sure I am as willing as anybody to extend a helping hand to them. But the de Salles will be desperately poor—as they all are—and very prickly to handle—as they are all equally proud. The *émigrés* I have met in London protest that they wish to earn their bread, but they have not a notion how to set about it. At most they are only able to teach French, or a stiff, outmoded form of foreign dancing. They are not at all liked."

"I pity them."

"Pity is the last thing they wish for or will tolerate. 'We have our lives, madame,' they will say with their formal curtsies and unbending bows. 'We are more fortunate than many of our fellow countrymen.' That they will starve trying to find means to preserve those lives appears to be of the smallest consequence."

It was at that moment that the door opened and Sir William appeared: he was in appearance an older edition of his son, and just now his face wore an extremely grave expression. With him there came the short untidy figure of Mr. Lingford.

"My dear," he said, "you know Mr. Lingford, do you not? And you, Drum, I feel sure you have met him more than once."

"Your servant, ma'am," said Henry Lingford, bowing to the lady and including Drum in his bow. "And yours, sir."

"Mr. Lingford has come to tell me that the body of a man has been washed up on the shore in Rydd: he and his grandson came upon it this morning. He thinks the man was French and has brought me a scrap of paper and a seal that was in a leather bag attached to the clothing. The paper has my name on it and the seal is undoubtedly that of de Salle."

His wife exclaimed. "You do not think that poor M. de Salle tried to row across in the fog and was drowned?"

"It may be so. I intend to accompany Mr. Lingford back to Rydd directly I have given directions to my clerk how to proceed with certain cases in my absence. In the meantime no doubt you will order refreshment for Mr. Lingford: I will leave him with you, my dear."

"Of course." She summoned the servant and gave the necessary orders and begged Mr. Lingford to sit down. "I am sorry you have had a journey on such an errand, sir, but sad as it is I cannot help hoping that the poor man is not Sir William's friend."

"I hope so too, ma'am." Mr. Lingford's voice was grim and Drum glanced at him quickly. From the look on the old gentleman's face it occurred to him that this had been no ordinary drowning: something else had happened that had made him come after his father.

"If you will excuse me, Mamma," he said, "I will accompany my father. I may be of some use to him."

"Do go with him, Drum." Left alone with Mr. Lingford while he drank his wine and munched the cakes that had been brought for him, Lady Connington tried to make conversation. "I hear you have your grandchildren with you, Mr. Lingford," she said brightly.

"Why yes." He cursed the gossip of a small town that would not let a man's private affairs alone. "They are in lodgings in Rydd. I am having my house put in order."

"To be sure." She was sympathetic. "Living alone as long as you have done, extra rooms will need to be opened up and aired for the young people and more servants engaged. Have you a good housekeeper, Mr. Lingford?"

He had to admit that he had no housekeeper at all.

"No housekeeper? That is very bad." She was more sympathetic still. "But I know how difficult it is in these days to find reliable and good servants. I have heard though that the blacksmith's sister, Mrs. Ellen Muspratt, is seeking a situation as housekeeper, and I believe she might be exactly the sort of woman that you require. You may remember her: she was a housemaid once years ago at Emmetts Hall. If I were you, sir, I would send for her without delay."

Henry Lingford found that he was being carried too fast along a road that he had no wish to travel. He had come to Meldrum on one errand only, to fetch Sir William to look at a dead Frenchman, and here was her ladyship arranging for him to open up rooms for his grandchildren and engage housekeepers. He thanked her, however, the manners he had learned with regard to his behaviour to a lady remaining with him, and applied himself to the wine and cakes, relieved when the door opened again to admit Sir William and his son, both ready for the five-mile ride back to Rydd.

Except for Charles the boatshed was empty when they arrived, the men who had been working there having slipped away directly they saw the post-chaise accompanied by Sir William and his son on horseback coming down the road to the harbour. Charles remained seated in the wood shavings, his hands clasped about his knees.

"Ah, Charles, you are still here." His grandfather's hand rested for a moment on the boy's shoulder. "I knew I could depend on you. Go to your dinner now, lad. Your work here is done."

Charles scrambled up, bowed to the two gentlemen and ran off, glad to be done with his vigil and not thinking he would be able to eat his dinner until he was out in the air and racing the fifty yards or so to the Bowery, when he suddenly knew how famished he was.

Henry Lingford drew back the sailcloth from the dead man's face. "He is almost unrecognizable," he said. "But you may know his features."

Sir William bent over the corpse and then drew back. "Yes," he said heavily, "that is de Salle." His eyes met Mr. Lingford's. "He did not drown, sir."

"No, sir. He was murdered as surely as if he had stayed to face the guillotine."

"Can you remember what the master of the *Turk* said when he returned without him?" It was the judicial tone of the magistrate that was speaking now and the old man did not meet his eyes.

"Why," he said in a hurry, "I told you, sir. There was a fog that came down suddenly in mid-Channel. As thick as your arm, Dury said: he could see nothing."

"And you say he is reliable?"

"As reliable as any of these men can be. He is a first class seaman, fore and aft. If he could have found him I would be ready to wager that he would."

"But somebody else found him instead, and having got him on board with what money he had been able to bring with him, that was the end of de Salle." The baronet's voice was edged with anger. "I'd like to lay my hands on the villain."

"You are not alone there, sir," said Drum. "What will you do?"

Old Lingford glancing from father to son saw the same look on each face and wondered if he had been mistaken in dismissing Drum Connington for a weak fop. There was an uncomfortable lack of weakness about him at that moment.

"I will see the Rector at once and have the body fetched to the church for burial," said Sir William abruptly. "When his family arrives they may wish to have him disinterred later and reburied in the French cemetery in London or elsewhere." He gave an exclamation of dismay. "The family! De Salle said in his last letter to me that they were to set off on May 26th —that is barely two weeks from today. I trust your man will find *them*, Mr. Lingford?"

"He will find them, I give you my word for that, Sir William." Henry Lingford's face expressed determination. "I shall tell Adam Dury what has happened to M. de Salle and that he is to find his family if he has to wait in the Channel twenty-four hours or more."

Drum Connington, watching the little scene, felt that perhaps Mr. Lingford was not quite as confident of the outcome as he sounded. It might, he thought idly, be an excellent thing if one were to make sure that his confidence in the man Dury were to be rewarded. And then he heard a small gasp beside him and turned to find Martha there.

She had come in so quietly that they had not heard her, and she was looking with horror and pity at the uncovered face of the Frenchman. He went forward and covered it quickly while his father went back to his horse: at the same moment Henry Lingford caught sight of his grand-daughter, and let loose his inner uneasiness over the whole situation on her head.

"What the hell are you doing in this galley, madam?" he demanded in a low voice, but not so low that Drum could not hear. "Have you come to pry, or are you after your brother? When will you learn to let him off a leading rein and allow him to grow up? There is no work for you here, damn you. Get you gone."

"I have looked on death before," she reminded him quietly, and Mr. Connington, rising to his feet, was surprised by her composure and, indeed, by her dignity.

"Charles is at the Bowery eating his dinner. He told me that you were here and I came to offer you dinner with us. If I have done wrong I beg your pardon. I had no wish to intrude." Her head moved in the slightest of acknowledgement to Mr. Connington and unsmiling she departed as quietly as she had come.

"You have a thoughtful grand-daughter, sir." Drum spoke abruptly, annoyed with the old man for his incivility.

"She is a termagant, that one," grumbled old Henry. Martha's offer had made him realize that he should have offered the two gentlemen a meal at Rydd House, just as he knew that it was impossible. When he thought of the old crone in the kitchen there and the kind of dinners that she served up to him he knew a sensation of shame. In the old days at Emmetts he had been able to invite friends in to dinner on any day of the week, and the kitchens there were full of their servants as well as his own.

While he stood unhappily silent Drum went out on to the quay to wait for his father there in fresher air, and he found his thoughts dwelling again with some surprise on Martha Lingford.

He did not know of one among the young ladies of his acquaintance who would not have seized the opportunity for swooning at the sight of the drowned Frenchman. But not Miss Lingford. She had stood very firmly on her own slender feet and she had answered her grandfather's attack on her with a composure that he had admired, albeit with a slight feeling of unwilling disapproval. It was singularly unwomanly of her not to have burst into tears or at least indulge in a mild fit of hysterics at the old man's rudeness, but she had been quite unmoved. "I have looked on death before," she had said, her eyes full of contempt. Hazel eyes they were: he had thought them to be dark before, but the light from the fitful sunshine from the sea dancing on the walls of the boatshed had turned them for a moment almost to gold. They had also been angry eyes, just as the set of her chin promised no womanly weakness. He did not know if he admired or resented her most: one thing was clear, however, that every time he met her she stayed in his mind to an annoying degree.

He walked along the quay, still thinking about her, while he waited for his father's return. An old man was seated on an empty cask mending a net: his attention was all for his work and yet Drum had the feeling that he knew everything that had been going on that morning.

As he stopped beside him he looked up, his eyes as blue as many seamen's are, as if during the years at sea they had caught its colour, and Mr. Connington recognized him with an exclamation of pleasure.

"Amos," he cried, "my dear old friend, shake hands with me! I shall never forget our fishing expeditions—you and me and Harry Redfern."

"Aye, Mr. Drum. They was good days." Amos shook hands solemnly and returned to his net. "I hear," he said carefully, "that Mr. Harry is to be the new Revenue Officer on the Customs cutter."

"My mother told me so this morning. I am very glad for Harry."

Old Amos did not appear to share his enthusiasm: he turned the subject rather quickly.

"Folks say there's another body been washed up this

morning," he said. "A Frenchie, so I'm told."

Drum reflected that news had always travelled fast in Rydd. He said slowly: "My father is much concerned. It happens to be a friend of his, do you see, and he had arranged for a boat to be sent for him."

"Aye," said Amos composedly. "The *Turk*. Adam Dury is the master of it."

"The *Turk*. That is the name of the boat." Drum wondered how much the old man knew about the business. "Is she in harbour now?"

"No, Mr. Drum. She left early on the tide and she won't be back I reckon until nightfall if then."

"I would have liked to see Dury," said Mr. Connington, frowning. "I hear that the *Turk* set out to meet my father's friend but that a fog came down in mid-Channel and they missed each other. As he would be bringing a fair amount of cash with him no doubt some other man picked him up, took the money and cut his throat."

"Cut his throat, Mr. Drum?" Amos had not heard that: he was considerably startled. "Why, how can you know that, sir?"

"You have only to look at the corpse," Drum said, watching the old man closely. "This was not drowning, Amos. This was a brutal murder." He could see a small body of men headed by his father and the Rector coming down the street towards the quay and the boatshed and he turned away to meet them. "It was a pity there was a fog that night," he said.

And then Amos spoke, apparently addressing the net he was mending. "There's fogs and fogs," he said. "And them as comes down in the Channel yonder is queerest of all. Some can come like a blessing and be nothing but gain—and others can act like a cloak to hide things as shouldn't be seen."

"Like the landing of good French brandy, Amos?" said Drum smiling. The blue eyes gave him a quick glance.

"Or like the murder of a Frenchman, Mr. Drum."

Seven

As Henry Lingford walked back to Rydd House through the town his thoughts went from the dead Frenchman to the days of his youth when a visit to Paris had been part of his education. He remembered the fine salons of the French aristocrats, the glittering French Court, the beautiful furniture and the rich hangings in the great houses, and from there his mind travelled on to the house where he lived now, a house that had fallen into such disrepair that the mending of its gateposts and its roof alone would not set it right.

Lady Connington had been right when she said that he needed a housekeeper. Somebody should certainly be there to clean the rooms and air the house so that at least that termagant at the Bowery would not be able to say that it was not fit for the children of gentlemen. He would like to have pretty Sukey and young Charles living there with him to bring it to life while as for their sister, if she was under his roof he would soon show her who was master.

The thought pleased the sadistic side of his nature and as he drew level with the blacksmith's forge he saw Goliath working there and stopped to speak to him about his sister Ellen Muspratt.

"I am told she is looking for a place," he said.

"Why yes, Mr. Lingford, sir." The big man left his hammering on the glowing iron, thrust it back into his furnace, and came out of the forge for a moment to talk to him.

"I am told she was a housemaid at Emmetts years ago?"

"She wur there ten years was Ellen. You may recall her, sir—a wonderfully ugly young woman."

Mr. Lingford said he did not recall her. He never remembered ugly women, were they housemaids or duchesses.

"She married from Emmetts," went on Goliath. "But her two children died of the smallpox and the poor soul lost her husband six months back from a low fever, and now she is left to earn her bread as best she may."

Mr. Lingford said that he needed a housekeeper at Rydd House and the smith gave him a shrewd glance, remembering how few women in the past had undertaken such a situation there and why. "I hope that my grandchildren are coming to live with me," went on Henry Lingford evenly, "and I have only an old woman to wait on them. The house is badly kept."

Goliath said that his sister was living in his house

in Rydd and that he would tell her to come and see Mr. Lingford, and Henry Lingford went home to eat the unappetizing dinner that the old woman had cooked for him, made more unappetizing still because it had been kept so long.

Ellen Muspratt came to see him the next morning. She was, he noticed, very ugly, but there was a wholesome cleanliness about her that was encouraging.

He took her over the house himself and listened wryly to her comments. The grid was broken in the kitchen, there were holes in the washing copper, and there was scarcely a skillet fit to use, nor a piece of crockery that was not cracked, and there were no saucepans.

"What are your sauces made in?" she wanted to know. "Without a saucepan?"

He could not tell her. The pantry too was in a shocking state. "And only half a sugar-loaf in the store cupboard, and that eaten by mice!" she exclaimed.

She agreed to come, however, at a wage of ten pounds a year, and she said she would come the next day, her brother being willing to move her few bundles to Rydd House. After she had gone he had great satisfaction in giving his old crone notice.

When his new housekeeper arrived he told her to go into the town and order what she wanted for his house, Ben Heavers taking her in the little cart. She brought back new sheets, and replaced a mattress in which the mice had made a nest.

When she had given him an account of what she had spent she asked him if he would engage more servants. "There was more than two score at Emmetts," she reminded him.

"I don't need half a score here," he said tersely.

"No, but you need more than two men, sir, and one of them Jonas Pegg."

"Pegg has been with me for years," he said defensively.

"And he is no less fond of drinking than he was, I'll lay," she said sharply. "You need three or four maidservants sir, if your young ladies are coming to live here."

"Well, see if you can find some country lasses who will work hard and know their place." He was unwilling to admit that he had not yet asked his grandchildren to share his house. He was strangely averse to doing so, knowing how he and Martha were at cross-purposes whenever they met.

And then the thought of the French refugees, due to arrive shortly, came to his mind. Could he not make them an excuse? Could he not offer them hospitality for a few nights in his house when they arrived, claiming that they would be too exhausted to travel the five miles to Meldrum?

It seemed an excellent solution to the problem and in the morning he set out for the Bowery and found a large woman with a basket on her arm starting out for the market.

He asked Mrs. Spry who she was and was told that she was Miss Lingford's maid.

"Huh!" Henry Lingford stalked past her into the little parlour where Martha was mending a tear in her brother's best jacket. "So you can afford to keep a servant?" he said.

Martha raised calm eyes to his face. "Good morning, sir," she said, getting up to drop him a small curtsey before returning to her sewing. "Yes. Betsy was with my mother when she first married and she became nurse to us all. I would not part with her for the world."

He scowled at her in silence and then his brow cleared. No doubt Mrs. Muspratt would find a use for her at Rydd House. "I have engaged a housekeeper to put my house to rights," he said abruptly. "And I hope that when she has done it will be one that you will not be ashamed to enter."

His irony left her unmoved and as she did not reply he went on angrily: "I wish to entertain friends there in the near future, and as there will be ladies among them I would like to have a lady in my household to be their hostess."

Again he waited, while scathing retorts came to her lips to be severely repressed. What was the sense after all in quarrelling with the old man by asking if his doxy would not be good enough for any lady of his acquaintance? Moreover, Sukey and Charles liked the old man, and she did not want to endanger their chances in the future. So she remained silent, and goaded by her lack of curiosity he burst out, "You do not ask me which lady I would like to play hostess in my house?"

"It is scarcely my business." The reply expressed an almost cruel unconcern, and he realized that he must employ different tactics if he wanted to get his way.

"Damn it, girl, will you come and stay at Rydd House for a few nights?" Her antagonism was so real that he dare not say what was really in his mind. "You can bring Sukey and Charles and your maid with you if you wish. My housekeeper will see that rooms are ready for you all. I know the house has been sadly neglected, but I am old, Martha, and it is not a man's work to see to his housekeeping."

She wondered if he were trying to win her sympathy and hardened her heart against him. She did not trust him an inch.

"I shall have to consider it," she said coolly. "I have been waiting to hear, sir, if you had received any reply to the letter I wrote for you to the lords of the Admiralty. I hope you did not put it on the fire, because that will mean that Charles will have to look for another school this summer."

"I have not received any reply yet." His impatience boiled over in an explosion of wrath. "God damn you, woman, why will you persist in being so unreasonable? I ask for a simple service—a mere couple of days' visit to my house—and you say you will 'consider' it. But you need not trouble yourself any further madam. The ladies I am expecting are friends of Sir William Connington's, who is a justice of the peace and will vouch for their respectability, and no doubt they will be able to put up with my housekeeper until he sends for them. They will be too tired—and possibly too seasick—to know where they are for a time. It would be an advantage to have somebody there to speak their lingo, but I daresay neither you nor Sukey know a word of French."

"French!" At last he had won her attention. She looked up from her work, her face alight with interest. "Do you mean that these people will have come over from France?"

"French *émigrés*." He nodded. "Poor devils—they are the family of the fellow who was washed up here a few days ago, and I'd hoped that as three are women

and there is a child among them I could provide a
lady to welcome them. But think no more of it. I daresay Sir William will send a carriage for them, and
another five miles or so on the road after all they have
been through will do no more to kill them than they
have endured already." As he reached the door she
stopped him.

"Wait!" she said. "I beg your pardon, sir. I did not
think—I did not realize—"

"That my friends could be so respectable?"

"Not that." But she flushed all the same. "Thank
you, we shall be pleased to stay in your house for
the time you mention, and indeed longer if it should
be necessary, to make your friends welcome in your
house and to England." She added after a moment,
"Sukey speaks French very well. They had a French
lady to teach them at her school in Bath. I can only
speak a few words I am afraid."

"It will be sufficient, no doubt." He did not show
her by a muscle in his face the triumph that he felt:
even her continued formal use of "sir" in addressing
him did nothing to destroy it. He would even the score
between them yet, once he had got her into his house.
When she was dependent on him for a home for her
brother and sister she would change her tune: there
would be no tantrums then. She would do as she was
told.

Old Amos's words had stuck in Drum Connington's
mind for some days after de Salle's body had been
found, and he wondered if there was any hidden mean-
ing behind them, and if, in fact, they contained a warning or a vague suspicion that the old man dare not say

outright. He thought he would seek out Harry and have a chat with him about the *Turk* and other matters, and the passing notion that he might see Miss Lingford again was also there at the back of his mind.

His Majesty's Customs boat the *Snipe*, a cutter of two hundred tons with a crew of thirty and a dozen guns, was in harbour on the day that he rode into Rydd. The tide was in and a few fishing boats were in the harbour, the smell of fish about them, and gulls screaming above as they waited for the guts to be thrown overboard.

Drum made his way to the *Snipe* and hailed her, asking if the captain was aboard. Harry came out himself on hearing who wanted him and took him down into his cabin with delight, offering him some excellent Hollands in which to drink his health.

"And to wish you joy of your command, Harry." Drum lifted his glass.

"Thank you." Harry laughed, his eyes bright with the mischief they had known at school. "I was told that Mr. Drum Connington was everywhere regarded as the *ton*," he said wickedly, "and I can see that my informant did not lie. The set of that coat would turn me green with envy, Drum, were I not convinced that I had a better one on my back."

"It is a pity there is no garden shed aboard," Drum said. "But as I am inclined to agree with you I will not challenge your sentiment." He came abruptly to more important matters than the set of a coat. "Harry, what do you know of the master of the *Turk*? It's a large fishing boat, and its captain is one Adam Dury."

Harry's eyebrows went up. "I know nothing about the man himself," he said. "Except that he is engaged

—as most of them are—in contraband. But the story goes that the owner of the boat is in fact old Henry Lingford."

"The devil he is!" Drum frowned. "That puts a very different aspect on the business. So, when my father asked Lingford if he knew a man who could be trusted to take a boat out to fetch de Salle he recommended the master of his own vessel!"

"Is there any reason why he should not have done so?"

"I suppose not."

"What is in your mind, Drum?"

"Something that old Amos said." He told his friend about the fog that had come down in the Channel making it impossible for Dury to find de Salle, and what Amos had to say about it.

"Old Amos always loves being mysterious," Harry reminded him.

"I know. All the same it would be satisfactory if we could discover from some other source that there was a fog in the Channel that night. We have got to remember that the *Turk* has been commissioned to go out and fetch de Salle's family next Wednesday se'en night, and I would not like them to run into another fog with equally disastrous results. My father is of the opinion that de Salle intended to bring several thousands of pounds in French money with him, and that Madame la Marquise will in all probability bring as much of her jewellery as she has been able to save."

"Indeed?" Harry's eyes were now as serious as his friend's. "Adam Dury is a scamp, unpopular with many, but women like him. His good looks and his animal spirits have got him into trouble more than once, but I suppose on the surface he makes his money from fishing as honestly as many another. If he engages in smuggling, so do others, and it is hard to catch them at it. He can be an insolent rascal when he likes though—a bit of a revolutionary from all accounts. He has been known to say in the Mariners' Arms yonder that he thought it was time England had a revolution 'same like they have in France'. But nobody takes him seriously."

"I thought you said you knew nothing about him?"

"I make it my business to find out what I can about gentlemen who engage in contraband. When they are not too blatant about what they are doing I leave them alone. But Dury makes it hard to do that sometimes."

Drum Connington returned to Meldrum without having set eyes on Miss Lingford, and with his mind no easier after his talk with Harry, and a few days later he rode again into Rydd. Half a mile outside the town his horse cast a shoe and he left him with the groom at the blacksmith's and walked on down to the quay.

The *Snipe* was on the point of sailing, but her captain saw him and waved to him. As Drum approached he came ashore for a moment and took him aside.

"I've made some enquiries," he said in a low voice. "And I've examined the log-books of various vessels that were in the vicinity of Boulogne on the date when de Salle should have been rescued, and according to them it was a clear night with moonshine."

"I thought as much." Drum frowned. "And yet if Lingford owns the *Turk* and sent Dury on that expedition the man would scarcely have murdered de Salle. What is your explanation of it, Harry?"

"I fancy there were some frigates out there at the time—French as well as English. My informant told me they appeared to be keeping watch on each other, and both French and English were watching the French coast. Now that we are at war with France his friends on this side may be making a final desperate attempt to rescue the little French king. There have been many plots afoot to smuggle him out of the Bastille as everybody knows. I daresay our friend Dury saw the frigates and not wishing to be blown out of the water in rescuing a French aristocrat, invented the story of the fog and set his helm for home."

"That could be the way of it." Drum pulled a face. "So poor de Salle was picked up by somebody else— not I think, by a French fisherman or his body would have been washed up on the other side."

"And if one of the French frigates had seen him he would not have had his throat cut. He'd have been taken back to Paris to have his head taken off in the way that seems most popular there at the moment." He turned back to his boat. "I must go, Drum. I am sorry I have not been a great deal of help to you over this business. But I have told my men to keep their eyes and ears open, in case they can discover a silversmith who has been changing a quantity of French money lately. Now that this murder has been discovered de Salle's louis d'or are going to burn a hole in his murderer's pocket and he will rid himself of them as quickly as he can."

He saluted and stepped aboard and in a few minutes the *Snipe* was under way: Drum walked back to the town in a thoughtful mood. There was no sign of the *Turk* in the harbour that morning, but in a very short while she was due to set out for her rendezvous with de Salle's family and he turned over in his mind a way that might help to ensure their safety.

He was walking up the High Street thinking how this could best be achieved when he met Martha Lingford and her sister coming out of a milliner's. He stopped to greet them and, with a saucy glance at her sister, Sukey asked him to admire her new bonnet. He obediently raised his quizzing glass to survey it and assured her that it suited her charmingly.

"Thank you." She blushed and smiled and he noticed that her sister looked as pleased as if he had been praising the hat on her own head and nobody in his right mind would have done that. In fact he averted his eyes from it hastily: it was from its battered brim to its draggled feather a most disgusting object.

There was however something on Miss Lingford's mind other than hats and bonnets that morning. "Mr. Connington," she said, "I cannot believe that my grandfather has carried out his intention of writing to Lady Connington. I know his dislike for writing letters."

"She has not told me that she has received a letter from Mr. Lingford," drawled Drum. "Was it an important letter, Miss Lingford?"

"It may be," Martha said gravely. "He thinks, you see, that your poor French family may be so exhausted by the time they arrive in Rydd that they would be grateful to rest at Rydd House for a little while before travelling on to Meldrum. My grandfather has a new housekeeper who appears to be a trustworthy and capable woman and my sister and I will be there to receive them. My sister speaks French," she added with a fond glance at Sukey.

How she loved that pretty, empty-headed little girl, thought Drum. He said that he was certain it would be a most excellent arrangement. "Especially if Miss Sukey is there to greet them in their own language," he added and Sukey blushed again and said she was afraid she had forgotten most of what she had learned in Bath.

So Sukey had been educated in Bath, he thought. And her sister? Had her impatience been learned in the harder school of adversity?

He walked back with the two ladies to the Bowery and at the quayside they were joined by Charles, who waved a catch of mackerel at them and said he had been out with Amos fishing.

"Do you know Amos, Mr. Connington?" he asked.

Drum said he had that pleasure, his eyes going past the boy to the harbour to see if the *Turk* had returned. But there was no sign of her, and although his journey might be said to be only partly successful he found satisfaction from the way Miss Lingford talked as they walked along, and the quiet friendliness with which she gave him her hand when saying goodbye.

Lady Connington was delighted to think that she would not be forced to wait up half the night or rise in the dawn to greet exhausted visitors.

"I daresay Rydd House will not be very clean," she told her son. "But that does not signify. French people never object to dirt. I remember when I was a girl and my parents were in Paris for a time—there was a craze for everything that was English there—my mamma always made my sister and me take posies with us when we went to the great French mansions to dine or to a ball. They were quite the dirtiest houses

I've ever known: the floors of the salons were so
filthy that my mamma had false hems put into our
gowns so that they would not touch them, while as for
the servants—they all had elaborately powdered hair
and red handkerchiefs round their necks, and when
they came near us to serve a dish or to pour a glass
of wine our little posies were more than necessary."
She made a little face. "Yes, I take it as very thoughtful
of Mr. Lingford. I did not think he had so kind a
nature."

Drum did not think so either and he wondered what
had been at the back of the old man's mind when he
had suggested it to his elder grand-daughter.

Eight

During the next few days when Ellen took over his
house and indulged in a frenzy of cleaning old Henry
Lingford was thankful to retire to the marsh with
Charles and his pistols.

"The house is in an uproar," he complained. Certainly with the washing of three months filling it with
steam from the new copper, and the windows set wide
and mattresses being beaten and carpets swept in nearly
every room, he was glad to escape and even to take
his grandson for small excursions into the surrounding
countryside in his little cart with Placid in the shafts.
Fidget did not take kindly to the cart.

Many miles they went, ambling slowly through
chalky roads, made almost impassable in parts by the
oxen-driven carts, and by flocks of sheep and herds

of cattle, besides the recalcitrant pig. Now and then the old man would stop outside an inn and go in with Charles for a draught of ale and a talk with the landlord. He was well known to them and he knew them all, asking after wives and children by name, exchanging bawdy stories, and proud of showing off his grandson.

At one inn, the Cock by name, in Routledge, a village on the borders of Kent and Sussex, the landlord showed him some French louis d'or that had been given him that week.

"We get a number of 'em from time to time," he said. "I dessay brought in by these French *émigrés*. A good few of 'em has landed in Hastings of late, so I hear. Rowed themselves across in some of their own boats, too."

Charles picked up one to examine it and Henry Lingford said he had had guilders given him in change for a ten-pound bank note in Rydd. "There are all kinds of foreign coins circulating these days," he added.

"I don't see why the Excise men are so interested all the same," said the landlord. "Hed one in here this week axing about French money. Hed I a quantity given me lately? Was it in gold or notes? Could I describe the man what paid 'em over? Now how can a body answer them questions this time of day? I told 'un I misremembered who'd given 'em to me, but there was a Frenchman staying here for one night on his way to London and maybe he paid his bill with 'em. I don't know."

"And how much do you pay out in English money for 'em?" asked old Lingford.

"That depends on who brings 'em in. For some it's never enough, that I do know and they say I'm cheating of 'em. But they allus says that: you can't be upsides with 'em. So I tells 'em to go to a silversmith with their French gold if they ain't satisfied and they are too thirsty to do that." His eyes met Henry Lingford's and a wink passed between them and Charles laughed with them.

On the morning of the day arranged for them to go to Rydd House one of the George Inn chaises arrived at the Bowery for Mr. Lingford's grandchildren, followed by his cart driven by Jonas and sent for Betsy and the luggage.

Charles had left the packing up to his sisters and to Betsy. It was a wet day and he made his way through the rain to the cottage where Amos lived beyond the drying yard for the nets. He kept them all waiting for fully half an hour and had a scolding from Betsy when he arrived.

"Your shoes not cleaned and all over mud, and your coat wet and smelling of fish," she said. "What Mr. Lingford's housekeeper will think of you I do not know."

They set off at once for Rydd House and although he had told his sisters a great deal about it, Martha was surprised at the difference in the place since she had last set foot in it.

The stone flags in the hall had been scoured and the shutters removed from the windows, and in their light the housekeeper who came to show them to their rooms was as neat and as clean and wholesome as the painted trollop had been otherwise. The bedrooms selected for the girls were in front facing the courtyard and the road, while Charles was above with the half-finished model of a frigate on a table under the window.

"The master thought you might like to have that in your room, Master Charles," Ellen Muspratt told him. "It was made by your great-uncle, his younger brother what went away to fight for the Jacobites in the rebellion of '45. He was only eighteen at the time, the master said: a mad rascal of a fellow. He was killed in one of the battles and the master said that it was a good thing that he was, or he would have been hanged along with the rest." She shivered. " 'Tis beautifully made, that little ship, and the master thought, seeing as you was going into the Navy you might like to finish it."

"If my hands are skilled enough." Charles examined the little vessel with delight while Mrs. Muspratt gave a glance at his tent bed and told Martha that she had had all the beds to pieces. "The mattresses and pillows have been out to bake whenever we have had sunshine," she said. "Good ones they are too, like all the Emmett mattresses and pillows and made of goose feathers. I have also had all the beds washed down with vinegar and water, to be on the safe side."

The dining-parlour, to the right of the entrance, was of a moderate size, being made darker by having its panelled walls covered from floor to ceiling in family portraits.

"There was a picture gallery at Emmetts," the old man said as they started on the excellent dinner that Ellen Muspratt had prepared for them. "But there were a number of Dutch and Italian pictures that were too large to be included here. So I sold them, only keeping the family likenesses—not that they are of much interest to anybody now."

"I think they are *very* interesting!" Sukey put out her

hand to him. "Some of the ladies' gowns are beautiful, Grandpapa."

"They are well done, though I sold the larger ones painted by Gainsborough. I do not like the way he paints the ladies: they simper too much. Now Lely—there is an artist for you. He shows almost more bosom in the ladies' gowns than the ladies themselves do today."

He glanced at the kerchiefs folded demurely into the tops of his grand-daughters gowns and his eyes met Sukey's and she laughed, while Martha took no notice, although a flicker of amusement appeared for a second in her face.

"I think," Sukey said, putting her hand in his, "that when you were young you must have been a very droll and delightful man."

"Thank you, my dear." He raised her hand to his lips. "I do not shock you then?"

"Shock me? Not in the least." Sukey laughed again and it was plain to Martha that already her sister could twist the old man round her little finger.

"The house looks nice since you have had Mrs. Ellen, and since the gates have been repaired," Charles said chattily. "When we first saw it that evening—of course it was getting dark and we did not see it properly—I was afraid that you might be a miser."

"A miser? God bless the boy, why should I be a miser?"

"There was an old gentleman in Crome who was a miser," Charles assured him solemnly. "He lived in a house as big as this and nobody thought he had any money until he died, and his two nephews found hundreds of guineas hidden in cupboards and under floorboards and in old trunks in the attics. They had terrible quarrels over it and they went to law about it, and in the end you will never guess what happened."

"The lawyers had it all?" ventured his grandfather.

"How did you guess that?" Charles was chagrined.

"It is the way those gentlemen have," said his grandfather dryly.

As the meal went on, he exerted himself to entertain Charles and Sukey, rather pointedly leaving Martha out of the conversation. It was not unexpected but at the same time it worried her a little. Her brother and sister were young and easily won over, and she wondered again why he had invited them there. She began to feel that the French *émigrés* might have been only an excuse.

Certainly the house was fit to receive anybody now. In the great parlour where she and Sukey repaired after dinner the portraits had been freed from their cobwebs, the glass chandeliers were out of their holland covers and filled with wax candles. The parlour was panelled as the dining-parlour had been, and Venetian mirrors hung on either side of the centre fireplace, reflecting light from the windows opposite. But as they sat on chairs covered in faded rose-red brocade playing cribbage with their grandfather after tea and coffee had been brought in the question remained unanswered at the back of Martha's mind. Why had all this been put in hand, and what was the reason for it? She was more certain than ever that old Henry Lingford would not have gone to such expense for nothing, and her uneasiness grew.

The *Turk* was not back until the morning of the day

on which the de Salle family was to be met and brought to England. There was a good catch of fish to be disposed of before the boat was put in order and the decks scrubbed down for the reception of the French party.

Drum Connington drove into Rydd that evening in his own carriage, leaving it to be put up for the night at the George Inn with his groom in attendance there.

He then walked on down to the quay where the fishing boat was riding easily on the tide and asked if he could see the master. Adam Dury put his head through the hatch and recognizing his visitor came up on deck, grinning.

"Why Mr. Connington, sir," he said. "Come aboard. We shan't be sailing for another few minutes yet."

"Thank you, I will." Drum stepped aboard the boat and followed Dury down into the small cabin where the *émigrés* were to be accommodated.

"Your rendezvous with M. de Salle's family is in the same area I take it?" he said.

"Aye. That's where I'll make for—west side of Boulogne." The man was almost insolently assured, and glancing at him Drum found it hard to trust him.

"You have a good name for seamanship in Rydd, Dury. If anyone can find them, you will. It was a pity you did not find M. de Salle."

"Aye." Dury shook his head. "But the fog came down so thick: maybe I did ought to have waited case it lifted, but I was afeared of being run down by some of them French boats. There've been a fleet of 'em out there lately—waiting for these so-called aristocrats I s'pose."

"But surely you know how to deal with such boats,

Dury? I know your guns will not be equal to taking on a frigate, but nobody need tell you how to avoid being taken by them surely?"

Dury grinned but his eyes were watchful. "Of course the fog was as bad fur them as it was fur me," he said easily. "Maybe the French gentleman was found by one of they ships and taken aboard to hev his throat cut and be thrown back into the water."

"How did you know his throat had been cut," asked Drum mildly.

"Crew told me," said Adam Dury quickly. "He was working in the boatsheds the morning the poor gentleman was found."

Drum thought it over. "But if these ships were standing close in to the French coast any body thrown into the sea would not have been washed up on this side."

The smile left Dury's face abruptly and he scowled, his eyes more watchful still.

"They wasn't as close as that to the shore. The larger boats can't get in anywheres near Boulogne. The water is too shallow for 'em."

"You managed to see the ships that night then?" Drum asked the question casually and Dury's scowl deepened.

"I didn't see none of 'em, but I guessed they was there. They've been there for weeks now, watching for Frenchies. It seems the French is murdering everyone over there and these here aristocrats is running like rats."

"And being murdered by rats this side," drawled Mr. Connington. He raised languid eyes to the other's face. "But I do not believe that M. de Salle was murdered by the French, Dury, and neither do you. I believe he was picked up near your rendezvous. You see, his pockets were slit and nothing was left on him to show who he was—except for a scrap of paper in a small leather bag sewn into his breeches. The man who murdered him for his money overlooked that."

Just for a moment he thought he saw dismay in the man's eyes and then Dury's chin went up truculently. "Well, it wasn't me nor none of my crew, sir. I tell you I stayed there as long as I durst and then I set sail for 'ome without 'un. It was a wasted journey."

"But in spite of that you are going out tonight to pick up his family." The drawl had suddenly gone and the words were more of a command than a request. "And to make sure of finding them I am coming with you."

"You sir?" The man was startled. "Why?"

"Just to make sure that there is no fog in the Channel tonight, perhaps." Having mounted to the deck again. Mr. Connington settled himself on a coil of rope at the top of the hatch and as he did so his coat fell open a little and Adam Dury had an excellent view of a pair of pistols that the gentleman was carrying with him.

Old Henry Lingford took Charles with him to the quay to see the *Turk* sail and missed it by half an hour. He came back in a fury and shut himself up in his little room with his guns and his fishing rods and refused to speak to anyone.

"What in the world is the matter?" the girls asked their brother. "What has happened?"

"He is angry because Amos told us that Mr. Connington had sailed with the *Turk*," Charles told them. "He says that Dury, the master of the boat, will think he don't trust him and that he asked Mr. Connington to go with him."

"Why should he think that?" asked Sukey innocently while Martha observed that she could see no reason why Mr. Connington should not go on the *Turk* to meet his friends. "There can be no harm in it surely?" she said.

"You know what Grandpapa is like," Charles said. "He flies into rages over nothing sometimes."

"I do not know what he is like," Martha said emphatically. "And neither do I wish to know. On the day that these French people leave Rydd House we shall move back to the Bowery."

"Then I hope they stay a long time," Sukey said rebelliously. "It is much nicer to live in a big house like this than to be hidden away in a pokey little cottage."

Tea was brought into the parlour and Sukey said she would see if she could not persuade her grandfather to come and play another game of cribbage, and she was successful: the old man allowed himself to be coaxed into a game although he said he was not going to wait up for their guests.

"Let Connington bring them here in his grand new carriage," he said. "He can knock the servants up when they arrive."

Supper came and the servants brought candles with it and the world outside the windows was suddenly quite dark. But the moon was rising and Martha wondered how the *Turk* was faring on its short voyage across the Channel. She wondered too why the fact that Drum Connington was on the boat had been a matter of such concern to her grandfather.

When they went up to bed later she saw Sukey into bed and then retired to her own room next door. She did not undress, intending to keep awake in case the poor fugitives arrived, but she was tired and dropped off at midnight into an uneasy sleep, waking at first light to hear the birds singing outside the closed shutters.

She sat up listening for sounds of arrival, but there were none, and she got up quietly, opening the shutters and bathing her face and hands in cold water from the ewer on the wash hand stand. Then she changed her gown for a morning one in brown cambric, brushed her hair and dressed it neatly, before leaving the room and going softly down the stairs.

Ellen and Betsy and Ellen's two young maids were astir, folding back shutters, opening windows, getting fires lighted in the great parlour and in the bedrooms that waited for the *émigrés* upstairs. A kettle was nearly boiling on the kitchen hob and cold meats were being set out with wine in the dining-parlour.

The front door was unbolted and Martha opened it and went out and up the path to the front gate, but the bend in the road by the thicket of trees hid the town from her.

She was going back to the house when she caught sight of a dilapidated old summer house, built in a corner of the wall like an old-fashioned gazebo, and high enough to command a view of the town.

The morning mists were clearing quickly and as she mounted the crumbling steps she found that she had a clear view of the road and Drum Connington's new coach with its team of horses was moving slowly towards them from the west gate. She ran back to the house to find Betsy and to tell her to run upstairs at once and wake Sukey and help her to dress.

"I can see the carriage on the road," she said. "They will be here directly and she is our interpreter. We shall be lost without her."

Nine

Once free of the harbour a brisk breeze caught the *Turk*'s sails and sent her along at a speed that pleased Drum: old Lingford had been right to recommend the boat, he thought, and her master, rascal as he was, knew his craft. It was not until after sundown that it occurred to him to think, rather wryly, that he had made himself a hostage for the safe voyage of a party of French people whom he had never seen, and he hoped they would be grateful for it.

The winking lights of Rydd had been lost to sight for over an hour when along the French coast a single light showed itself, and Dury ordered the *Turk* to be put about, announcing surlily that they had reached the rendezvous.

The sails were lowered, the boat rode at anchor, and

the single light showed itself twice: Dury produced a long black lantern from the hold and taking a shutter from its shaft signalled back. The single light replied with three short signals and then stopped abruptly, perhaps because of sundry dark shapes far off towards Boulogne.

They had to wait for another hour before a small boat arrived, pulling wearily out to them with two men at the oars and three women and a child hidden under sacking in the bottom.

The *émigrés'* journey from Paris had been a nightmare one, culminating in a wait for a boat in Boulogne, being watched and followed and almost apprehended at the last. If it had not been for the brother of the child's *bonne* who swore solemnly that they were his wife's relatives from the country, and that the child had smallpox, that might turn out to be the plague, they must have been betrayed and dragged back to Paris.

As Drum helped them on board they scarcely knew if they were among friends or still with their enemies, and Mr. Connington's pistols did not encourage them. They wondered at first if they might be attacked, and it was only when he spoke to them in halting French, reassuring them and giving them rum to warm them, because on that summer night they were shivering and the dawn was blowing up cold, that they knew they had been saved after all.

They arranged themselves in the cabin below, directed to seats there, the *bonne* settling herself on the floor with the child in her arms, the two ladies sitting side by side, the older one bolt upright, her dark eyes everywhere, the younger one torn between caring for her dead husband's mother and his little daughter. The young man, her brother-in-law, tried to exchange a few words in English with Drum, encouraged by his smiling friendliness.

He asked if he had met his father, and whether he would be at Rydd to meet them. Drum had a memory of the man with his throat cut and thought it best not to understand. He explained that they were to go to a house in Rydd first to rest and that Sir William Connington intended to fetch them the following day, but the detailed explanation became too much for his French and the young man's English and all that he managed to impart was that they were among friends and all was well. Reassured the young man joined his family below and left Mr. Connington to his seat on the coil of rope and his study of the sky, where dawn was sending a first pearly light into the eastern horizon.

It had been daylight for two hours or more by the time the *Turk* came to rest in the small harbour, and the exhausted people on board were helped on to the quay and into Mr. Connington's carriage that had been waiting for them since first light.

When Jules de Salle would have paid Dury, however, Drum stopped him peremptorily. "My father will settle with Dury later," he said and mounting to the coachman's seat he gathered the reins into his hands.

Adam Dury watched them go with murder in his heart and said exactly what he thought of French *émigrés* and of these in particular, including in it his opinion of Drum Connington and his father.

For the travellers the first sight of Rydd House was a vision of Paradise. The high walls, the gate set open to welcome them, the path to the door through an

English garden, and the two young Englishwomen waiting to greet them with outstretched hands and soft sympathy, and one of them moreover speaking fluent French, made them feel that they had really reached safety at last. Everything was ready to receive them, even to warmed milk for the child—a little girl of three years old who stared at Sukey with great dark eyes and allowed her to take her from her nurse's arms without any outcry at all.

Jules de Salle, staring at Sukey as if she were an angel from Heaven, told her that she was very like his younger sister, and the child believed it was Marianne come back again. On further enquiry Sukey learned that his sister had refused to leave her husband and had been guillotined with him in Paris.

Martha, to whom this information was relayed later, was appalled. Death by guillotine seemed to be accepted by these aristocrats with resignation. In Somerset they had been protected from violence and murder: it seemed that only when they had left that haven for their grandfather's house in Rydd that such things invaded their peace of mind.

Drum Connington, having seen his party into the house, departed to the George to get himself shaved and to eat a leisurely breakfast before returning to discover when Mr. Lingford would wish their guests to be fetched to Meldrum.

After a breakfast that they were too exhausted to eat the *émigrés* had gone thankfully to their beds and were still there when Mr. Connington arrived. Now he was shaved and his hair restored to its fashionable cut and his linen once more immaculate, he had no objection to calling upon old Lingford again, odd fish as he was, for the sake of improving his acquaintance with his elder granddaughter.

Mr. Lingford had breakfasted and was in a better temper than he had been the night before, and welcomed him mildly, asking why he had thought it necessary to go out on the *Turk*, and adding a hope that it was not because he mistrusted her master.

"On the contrary," Drum said, drawling a little, "Mr. Dury appears to me to be an excellent seaman, sir. But it occurred to me that it might be comforting for our guests to have a member of my father's family aboard." The old man appeared to be satisfied with this explanation and Drum followed it up by giving him a letter that had been waiting for Mr. Lingford at the George.

He glanced at it and then put it on one side and sent the servant for Martha. She came in a hurry and stopped on the threshold at seeing that he was not alone. The immaculate Mr. Connington and his quizzing glass disconcerted her a little.

"Mr. Connington has come to enquire after our *émigrés*, my dear," said Henry Lingford. "Lady Connington would like to know when she is to expect them at Meldrum."

"They are very exhausted, sir." Martha's eyes met Drum's impersonally, almost as if he were a stranger. "They are all sleeping now, and the little girl is too tired to be moved for a little while. I think my grandfather should keep them here for a few days if Lady Connington has no objection."

"None in the world." It would give him an excuse to call again in a few days and discover if he could why she had become so distant after the friendliness of their last meeting.

"Mr. Connington brought a letter for me which may upset your plans," Mr. Lingford said, handing it to her. "You had better open it at once and make sure that I do not put it on the fire." He added ironically: "My granddaughter does not trust me, Mr. Connington."

And with good reason, thought Drum, but he merely bowed and waited while Martha broke the seal and unfolded the letter, and as she read it he saw her face flush and her eyes sparkle and he told himself, "By God, when she forgets to frown she's prettier than her sister, damned if she ain't!"

"It is about Charles, sir," she said, handing it to the old man. "It is from the lords of the Admiralty. He is to go to the school at Portsmouth without delay. Oh, is not this wonderful news?" She suddenly remembered their visitor. "Forgive me, Mr. Connington, but I must find my brother at once."

She ran from the room and came back almost directly with Charles.

"We will set out on Saturday—the day after tomorrow," his grandfather told him when he had been shown the letter. "Your sister may start packing your trunk at once."

"I beg your pardon, sir." Martha's frown returned, her excitement suddenly quenched. "*I* will conduct Charles to Portsmouth."

"You will do nothing of the sort." The old man scowled at her while Drum Connington watched, immensely amused by the clash of wills that had suddenly arisen between them like a storm out of a summer sky. Certainly where Martha Lingford was life could never become a bore.

"Then I will come with you," she said setting her chin.

"Nor that either. I do not wish for your company and neither does Charles. This is one occasion when he will not be managed by a petticoat. I shall take him to Portsmouth myself and alone. Let that be understood if you please."

Martha stood for a moment scarlet with anger quite forgetting their visitor and then she whisked out of the room taking Charles with her.

"Would you like my father to send for our friends sooner?" asked Drum, concerned. "I do not suppose they will suffer by a removal to Meldrum on Saturday."

"It would be the wiser course, although the girls will look after them, and I daresay Sukey will not find it amiss to have a handsome young man to talk to in a lingo that her sister will not understand!" Old Lingford cackled with sudden laughter and Drum smiled faintly, wondering why the old devil had got his knife into his elder granddaughter. It might be interesting to find out.

In the meantime Betsy, between confused directions from Martha to sort through Charles's clothes, was full of a story that Ben had told her, having had it from Mr. Drum Connington's groom.

"It seems there was an argument between Mr. Connington and the master of the *Turk* before they sailed," she told her. "Some say Mr. Connington had to show Adam Dury a pistol before he'd take the boat out with him abroad. Real angry he were, and 'tis said Dury is saying as Mr. Lingford was at the bottom of it and that

he'll be even with him for it. But Ben says he's no call
to talk like that seeing as it was Mr. Lingford what
had the boat built for him in the first place, which is
the first I heard of it." She broke off suddenly. "Mind
you, that's only gossip. You can't believe all you hear."

"No, you cannot, Betsy, and you know my opinion
of gossip." Martha spoke severely, inwardly longing to
hear more and when Betsy left the room for a moment
she asked Charles if there was any truth in the story
and if that was why their grandfather had been so
angry on learning that Mr. Connington had sailed in
the *Turk*. "Does the boat really belong to him,
Charles?" she asked.

He was slightly embarrassed and said that he did
not know, that Ben did not know what he was saying.

"I think he knew very well what he was saying,"
Martha said disappointed in her brother. He had always been so open with her and now that he was at
Rydd House she wondered if he was learning devious
ways from the old man downstairs. When Betsy came
back she left them and made her way slowly to the
library where she found Mr. Connington on the point
of leaving.

She apologized for her abrupt departure and expressed a hope that he had had refreshment offered
him before his drive home.

"Your grandfather has been hospitality itself, thank
you, but I will not wait." He added, smiling: "Will
you not walk to the gate with me?"

"Thank you." She accompanied him along the path
and acting on impulse told him what she had heard
from Betsy. "Does my grandfather own the *Turk*?" she
asked.

His reply came cautiously. "I believe he had it built for Dury. I have heard so."

She was silent for a moment and then she asked, "Why did you sail on the *Turk*, Mr. Connington?"

He was disconcerted and his drawl came back. "Shall we say that I was concerned for the safety of our friends?"

"Their safety, Mr. Connington?" Troubled hazel eyes were raised to his. "In what way did you think you could protect them?"

Damn the girl, why could she not accept what a man said, like most of her sex? He tried to hedge, his drawl becoming more pronounced. "We are at war with France, Miss Lingford: one cannot dismiss that fact from one's mind. There were five men on board the *Turk* and I made another in case of attack from any French vessel that might wish to know our business there."

"And so you risked your life for your father's friends?" She still sensed that there was something that he had not told her, that she did not understand.

"Oh come, Miss Lingford, it was not as bad as that!" He laughed lightly and placed his hat with its smart buckle firmly on his freshly dressed hair. "Life would be a great bore if one did not take a few risks sometimes, and I assure you there was very little danger to anybody."

She watched him climb to the box of his grand new carriage and move off down the lane and then she returned slowly to the house, where the *émigrés* were still sleeping off their exhaustion and even the little girl had cried herself to sleep, and applied herself to the more pressing problem of her brother's handkerchiefs and shirts.

Until Saturday she was forced to neglect their guests in her efforts to see that Charles would go to Portsmouth with an adequate supply of clothes, and left their entertainment to Sukey and their grandfather, but by Friday night all was completed and Charles's trunk was packed and ready for an early start in the morning.

When she got to bed on Friday night Martha found herself too tired to sleep: the numbers of Charles's garments revolved incessantly through her mind and presently she remembered that she had left her pocket book in the parlour. Being in no mind that her grandfather should take possession of it, she went downstairs with a candle to fetch it.

The house was very quiet, the candle making a small pool of light as she moved across the hall, and then as she reached the parlour door she heard voices coming from her grandfather's little room beyond the dining-parlour.

She fetched the pocket book from the writing-table where she had left it and halted a moment in the hall listening.

She recognized one of the voices as her grandfather's but the other she did not know at all. It was a rough voice and she fancied its tone was slightly threatening and blurred by drink, and for a moment she wondered if she should rouse one of the servants.

Mr. Lingford was speaking quite quietly, however, as if he knew his visitor well and she did not wish to bring his anger on her head by interference, however well meant it might be.

So she clasped her little pocket book in her hand

and went back to bed: it was only later that she was to remember the incident and the voice of the midnight visitor.

Adam Dury's accustomed knock on his window had brought old Henry Lingford to the door that opened into the yard and the man walked past him with scarcely a word of greeting.

"I've come for my money," he said truculently, seating himself in one of Mr. Lingford's chairs with his great hands squarely on his knees. "The money you owe me for bringing your fine French friends ashore, and I reckon they're all here, ain't they?"

"They are here, Adam, thanks to you." Mr. Lingford unlocked a drawer and took from it five pounds which he put into the man's hand. "That is for last Wednesday's work," he told him. He took another five pounds from the drawer and added it to the first. "And that is to pay you for the wasted journey you had before."

Adam Dury took the money without thanks and if Henry Lingford had hoped to placate him by the extra money he failed.

"Then that's the end of our business, isn't it, Mr. Lingford?" he said. "You owe me nothing and I owe you nothing. You paid for the *Turk* ten year ago and I reckon I've paid for her with measure to spare. Haven't you had the half of every cargo from a boat that cost you no more than fifty pound, and with no risk to yourself neither? But I'm going to sail on my own from this day forward, Mr. Lingford, and nobody is going to give me orders no more. The last order you gave was when you sent Mr. Meldrum Connington to board my boat on Wednesday last. From now on I say who is going to sail in the *Turk*, nobody else."

"I did not send Mr. Connington, Adam. He went without my knowledge. But where was the harm in it? He only wished to meet his father's friends. No harm could come of that."

"Then what did he mean by saying he was coming to see there was no fog this time? Does he think he's God that he can control the weather?"

There was a little silence and then Mr. Lingford said in an altered voice, "He meant nothing Adam. You are too ready to take offence."

"Wouldn't you take offence if you was called a murderer to your face?"

"Mr. Meldrum Connington has been away from Kent for some time. He don't know the people of Rydd as I do, or he would never have said such a thing to you. The new Revenue Officer is a friend of his—they were at school together in Rydd so I'm told—and I daresay he's been enquiring about fogs in case one was likely last Wednesday night. He don't know as you and I know that fogs can be patchy, and where one stretch of water is clear another may be as thick as a blanket. Take no heed of him: he'll be off to Gloucestershire when the mood takes him." He paused. "I am taking my grandson to Portsmouth and leaving him at a school there. I am leaving tomorrow and in my absence you may use the outhouses as usual, but when I return you must find another hiding place. The boy's eyes are sharp enough but his elder sister is a she-devil. If there is anything to be seen she will see it and she is not likely to keep a still tongue in her head."

Somewhat reassured Adam took the tankard of ale

that Mr. Lingford drew for him from the barrel in the corner and went his way, working along the footways across the marsh until he reached a group of men who were busy unloading a great many casks from a boat on the far side of the shingle bank.

In his little room Henry Lingford sat by his guttering candle turning things over in his mind. Ten years ago when he had had the *Turk* built for young Adam Dury he had been attracted by the boy's fearless disregard for law and order, an attitude that was very much in tune with his own. He had put him in charge of the boat not only as a gesture of contempt for the hypocritical citizens of Rydd, who were never averse to trading in contraband goods on the quiet, but also from a half-crazy inner desire to score off his own son.

For ten years their partnership had flourished, and if at times he became aware that the rules that governed it were subtly changing and that in fact, from being his man, Dury was becoming his master, it did not worry him a great deal until young Charles had come to Rydd.

Old Lingford thought of the boy he had known since last April and compared him with the man he had befriended over the past ten years and he knew that Adam Dury had lost his attraction and that it was Charles who now filled his thoughts.

Surely Dury and his band would see that he had to close Rydd House to them in the future? With more servants to the place and young people there anything stored in outhouses would be discovered immediately and he was getting too old to take such risks: there was no longer any pleasure to be found in flouting the law. With France closing her doors to English goods because of the war and the increased penalties Pitt was imposing on this side of the Channel the risks would increase with illicit trading and he wanted a quiet life at the end of his days.

One remark of Dury's stayed with him however as he went upstairs to bed. Why had Drum Connington said that he wanted to make sure there was no fog in the Channel that night? Had he heard something from Harry Redfern that had aroused his or his father's suspicions?

They could not suspect Adam Dury of having murdered de Salle surely? Adam might be a rascal but he was not such a black-hearted one as that. Besides, had he not personally recommended him to Sir William? Adam knew that, and for all his revolutionary ideas he would not be stpuid enough to put his neck into that sort of a noose. Unless de Salle had brought a great deal of money aboard.

Times were hard in England and the poor were starving for bread. It might have been wiser to send a man with less revolutionary ideas to save a rich Frenchman with a load of gold.

His thoughts shied away from the notion as surely as Fidget would shy at a shadow in the road, and like Martha he found it difficult to sleep for what remained of the night.

In the morning, after the Meldrum coach had arrived to take their French guests away and a Rydd chaise appeared in its place to conduct Charles and his grandfather on the first stage of their journey along the coastal road to Portsmouth, the old man told Martha that he would be obliged if she and her sister would remain at Rydd House until his return.

"I do not anticipate being back until the end of next week," he told her. "And I shall expect to find you here when I return."

"But I have sent word to Mrs. Spry to expect us to dinner today." Martha was dismayed.

"Then you must send your Betsy to tell her that you will not be returning for another week or fortnight." The old man's manner was peremptory. "Her cottage is isolated enough, beyond the boatshed and the harbour. I do not wish you and Sukey to be there at the moment. That is an order, Martha, and you will obey it—for your own safety and that of your sister. And another thing," he added as he prepared to follow Charles into the chaise, "if you venture into Rydd you will take Jonas with you, and your rambles along the shore must cease until after my return."

Only one explanation for his sudden concern for them seemed reasonable. "Are you afraid that somebody might attack us?" she asked.

"While you are under my roof you will not go abroad unless you have a servant with you," he said shortly. "Such rambles may be permitted in the country lanes of Somerset, but not here in Rydd and on the marsh. The friends and relatives of young ladies who live in Rydd are careful of their safety."

And then he kissed Sukey on the lips, extended two fingers to Martha, and getting into the chaise beside Charles was driven rapidly away.

Ten

On Monday morning Lady Connington came to call upon Martha and her sister.

"First of all, my dears," she said, "I am to thank you for your kindness to our poor *émigrés*. They are loud in your praises—at least I believe that is what they wish to say in the midst of their lamentations. My husband is concerned as usual with the justice room and my son is no help to me. He does nothing but take M. de Salle off to shoot pigeons. Which brings me to the object of my visit this morning."

Here she paused, studying Martha and Sukey reflectively. The elder girl had more sense, she thought, but how lovely the younger one was, with that curling hair and enormous blue eyes. She had a sweet manner too, unlike the stiffness of her sister.

"It seems that Mme de Salle's little grand-daughter, Thérèse, has taken a great fancy to your sister, Miss Lingford, and I understand that she can speak French." Her ladyship's smile was all for Sukey. "So I have come to beg her to take pity on our English lack of languages and visit us as long as our poor *émigrés* remain at Meldrum. They intend to be there until Mme. de Salle hears from her sister who is in London. She is hoping she will have accommodation for them all in her house—a small one, I believe, in the village of Chelsea. That is to say it has been a village but of late is become sadly urbanized. In fact, at the rate houses are being built in London it will not be long before streets of them spead to every surrounding village." She turned to Martha. "What do you say, Miss Lingford? Will you spare your sister to help us out of our difficulties?"

Martha accepted the invitation for her sister with pleasure, all the more because she saw that Sukey was delighted: it would be an excellent thing, she thought, for her to see such a place as Meldrum—equal, she had been told, to Emmetts in its heyday. It was the sort of residence she had planned for her pretty sister when they left Somerset.

"Then that is settled," said Lady Connington with satisfaction. She whisked Sukey away with her before either girl could draw breath, promising to send for Sukey's clothes and maid that evening. As she drove back with her captive to Meldrum her ladyship reflected with some satisfaction that Drum had kept remarkably quiet about the younger Miss Lingford's looks. Could it be that he was taken with her, she wondered? It had not escaped her that his visits to the little town often led him to Rydd House and he did not dismiss such visits as being a dead bore. She would know Sukey better after her stay at Meldrum, but in the meantime she was very favourably impressed with her first meeting with the girl and with her artless conversation as they travelled through the lanes together.

Betsy helped Martha to pack up a trunk full of clothes for her sister, including in it several favourite gowns of her own that Sukey had worn happily in the past.

"It is a very good thing that her ladyship did not want two interpreters at Meldrum," she told Betsy as they packed. "For both of us to appear suitably dressed would not have been possible, and one with a good selection of gowns will be much better. Fetch my blue bombazine, Betsy. We will pack that in the top of the trunk. And I will put in our mother's jewellery—the gold necklace and the pearl ear-rings will look lovely on Miss Sukey."

"Miss Sukey looks lovely in everything she wears," said Betsy. She had respect for Miss Lingford but Sukey was her favourite just as Charles was her darling. "He told me he would not go to sea for three years," she said later while they waited for the carriage that was to take Betsy to Meldrum. "And only three weeks' holiday in the year. I reckon he won't like that, Miss Lingford."

"But he can take those three weeks when he likes," Martha said consolingly. "And discipline will not hurt Charles. I am glad though he did not take his pistols with him." The case of pistols was on a table just inside the parlour door and she opened the box and took one out gingerly.

"Oh, Miss Lingford, dear, do put it back!" cried Betsy in terror. "It may be loaded—it might go off. Pray put it back."

Martha put it back. "I do not see why it should be loaded," she remarked. "They have only been used for shooting out on the marsh and Mr. Lingford always cleaned them afterwards."

For the next day or two after Sukey had gone Martha was busy superintending the household at Rydd House. She was glad that Betsy and Ellen had approved of each other but she looked forward to returning to the Bowery and kindly Mrs. Spry when her grandfather returned. She was surprised therefore when she had a caller on the second day after Sukey had gone.

"My mamma is extremely anxious about you, Miss Lingford," drawled Mr. Connington, looking rather more bored than usual. "She has learned from your sister that there is no other lady to keep you company here at Rydd House and she has written to the Rector's wife to suggest that she should invite you to stay at the Rectory while your grandfather is away. I am the bearer of a letter from Mrs. Hyde in which she says she will be happy to welcome you at the Rectory today."

"Then I will trouble you, sir, to take my compliments and thanks to Mrs. Hyde and to tell her that I am perfectly content to be here alone in my grandfather's absence." Martha spoke sharply, annoyed with her ladyship for her interference. Then she added more quietly: "It is very kind of Lady Connington to take so much trouble on my behalf, but I have been accustomed to take care of myself and others since I was twelve years old, and the absence of any other lady does not trouble me at all."

"Miss Sukey said that you would be annoyed," he said and there was no boredom now in the eyes that rested on her as he weighed up the ability of which she boasted before coming to the conclusion that she was right. "In fact she said that any intruder who "took on"—that was her expression—her sister Martha would be a very brave man." He saw her flush and she looked at him quickly and then she flushed again at his amusement. "I did not know you were reckoned by your family to be such a dragon, Miss Lingford."

She put up her head. "And I do not know that it is a crime for a woman to be independent, sir. In fact if more ladies were to follow my example it might be better for them." The Rector had brought his wife and three badly behaved children to call on her at the Bowery and she had no wish to improve on the acquaintance. "Mrs. Hyde is so meek and acquiescent that if I had been her husband I would have throttled her long ago."

He laughed outright and after a moment she laughed with him unwillingly. "It is a dead bore for you to have had such an errand thrust upon you," she said. "I will detain you no longer."

He could find no excuse to stay and he went his way, slightly bewitched by this tempestuous young woman who was afraid of nothing and in awe of nobody. He called at the Rectory and delivered her message, which was received with relief by the Rector's wife, who, poor soul, was already over-burdened with her household and her children, and as he was leaving he saw Harry Redfern coming up the street.

He handed the reins to his groom and swung himself down. "Harry," he said, walking with him a little way up the street so that his groom should not hear. "Old Lingford is away until Saturday at soonset and Miss Lingford will be alone at Rydd House. I am—that is my mother is concerned for her safety in the old man's absence. It would be a kind act if you could employ a few men to keep a watch on the place for the next few nights in case any ruffians should be surprised by the young lady while they are visiting the barns and out-houses there."

Harry said it was well known that old Lingford's place had been used for years by smugglers coming across the marsh. "We know it and I am sure your father knows it, Drum, but short of catching the men red-handed and involving the old man in the business, there is nothing we can do to stop it. If he is away however it would be the very thing, and we may be able to get our hands on to some of the gang that uses Rydd House. It could then be said that Henry Lingford knew nothing of it and we would save him and his grand-children from embarrassment."

Mr. Connington said that his mind—or rather that Lady Connington's mind—would be considerably re-lieved and asked if anything had been heard of any unusual amount of French money being exchanged in the district.

"Not yet," his friend told him, "but I do not despair. It has to be done carefully—casually as one might put it. My men are suspect, and though they have the entry where another would not, tongues are not loosened easily in front of them."

"That I can understand." Mr. Connington frowned. "Ah well, I will get back to Meldrum and discover if my young French friend is out of bed yet and willing to come pigeon shooting again before dinner." His air of boredom returned, he went back in a leisurely fashion to the curricle, examined a wheel that had mud thrown over its bright paint, and then getting easily into the coachman's seat he gathered up the reins, lifted a hand in farewell to his friend, and moved off up Castle Street to the open country and Meldrum beyond.

Harry Redfern watched him go with a smile. He wondered if the great Drum Connington had at last lost his heart to a young woman who was earning the reputation for being the most unapproachable young lady in Rydd. He had not been at all taken in by Drum's reference to his mother's concern for Miss Lingford. He did not think her ladyship would give a fig for her safety.

That night the young lady in question, having routed Mr. Connington, his mother and Mrs. Hyde, went up to bed for the first time with an inclination to listen for noises outside as well as within the house.

She saw no reason to be nervous, she scorned timorousness in others and had never given way to it herself. But because of Mr. Connington's visit that morning she found herself listening, and once in the night she woke up thinking she heard a shot near at hand.

She got out of bed and went to the window and unfolded a shutter. It was moonshine outside and she could see nothing in the lane, but far away she thought she could hear the sound of running feet, and then, across the marsh a light flickered and disappeared.

In the morning she asked Jonas if he had heard anything in the night as the servants' rooms faced on to the stables and coach-houses.

"No, miss, I ain't 'eard nothin'." His normally stupid face became slightly more stupid. "Maybe it was a smuggler or two coming across the marsh. A lot of that sort of thing goes on nights, and I've a fancy the Excise men were about. They're allus after they, but they don't catch 'em." He grinned. "You don't want to take heed of no noises you hear night-time on the marsh."

Martha was relieved that he took it so calmly: it appeared that she must get accustomed to such things while she was at Rydd House and she wondered how deeply her grandfather was involved in such things. She thought with relief that it could not be many more days before she was back with dear Mrs. Spry in the peaceful little Bowery.

She determined to waste no more thought on Mr. Connington. She did not like the man—he was too fond of laughing at her—and she had no patience with young men who wore a perpetual air of boredom. Moreover he had a great deal of money to spend, and while she was happy for little Sukey to enchant such people she had no desire to mix with them herself. She wished that Drum Connington did not find it so amusing to visit Rydd House.

Henry Lingford returned at the end of the week: he told her after close questioning on her part, that Charles was happy to take up his residence at the school, that his schoolmates appeared to be a friendly crew, and that he had every hope that his grandson would settle down there.

Martha said she was glad to hear it. "I am packed,"

she told him, "and though Sukey is at Meldrum, directly the French *émigrés* go she will join me with Betsy at the Bowery."

"What is this?" He stopped short. "Is Sukey not here?"

"No." She told him of Lady Connington's request for Sukey's help with her visitors, and he frowned over it and then he laughed.

"So the great Drum Connington has an eye on Sukey, has he?" he said. "Is that it?"

Martha said she thought Sukey was at Meldrum purely because she could speak French so well.

"If they only want her as an interpreter," her grandfather said dryly, "that young Frenchman is quite able to translate into English everything his mother and his sister-in-law say. No, my dear, there is more to Sukey's visit than that. Well, if Connington has taken to her so much the better. It will be a fine match for her, and she is pretty enough to attract any man, young or old."

It had not occurred to Martha until then that Drum Connington could be attracted to her sister, but although it was the kind of match that she had always dreamed of for her, she could not believe it possible, perhaps because she did not think such a man suited to Sukey. And then all thought of her pretty sister's matrimonial future went out of her mind as her grandfather said that he would be obliged if she and Sukey would regard Rydd House as their home in future.

"Our—home?"

"Why not? I believe that was your object when you first came to Rydd."

But they had not known that their destination would be Rydd House: in their minds had been their father's description of Emmetts, that lovely house that was no more.

"You will have a roof over your heads," he went on. "And good food in your stomachs. And if you were not extravagant no doubt I could find a little money for gewgaws. And when Sukey marries—as undoubtedly she will because she is far too pretty to remain single for long, though I hope it won't be to that stick Connington, rich as he is—then I daresay you and I will settle down here with a kind of truce between us."

"A truce?" She did not understand.

"Yes, my dear, a truce, for the sake of Sukey and Charles, and because we should be to some small extent dependent on each other, you on me for your keep and that of your family, and I on you for company."

"Company?" She felt stupid standing there repeating everything he said, but the dismay she felt at the prospect he placed in front of her prevented her from giving him a more sensible answer.

"Yes, I said company." He grew impatient. "Come, Martha, it is unlike you to be dull-witted. I'll confess that before you came to Rydd I did not think I should ever yearn after my own kin again, but I had not seen Sukey, neither had I met young Charles." He smiled and there was pride in his face, and for the first time since she had met him Martha felt herself soften a little. She frowned, considering the problem, and he saw the frown and said,

"Maybe even you and I would appreciate one another better if we saw more of each other. I would be

glad of your company, Martha. It has come upon me
lately that I am growing old."

And whose fault was it, she asked herself, that he
had been alone so long, with only the women from the
town to keep him company?

From childhood however her family's moves from
lodging to lodging in the wake of her father's regiment
had instilled in her a fear of debt that remained with
her still. Captain Lingford had never attempted to give
up the life of luxury in which he had been born, and
whenever they moved his creditors would come to
demand their money. And although the charm he
exerted might quieten some, in the end he had to
apply to his father-in-law to settle his bills.

When old Joseph Honeyman died he left three
thousand pounds to each of his daughters, Alicia and
Deborah, saying that they needed it more than their
brothers, and Captain Lingford had promptly sold his
commission and used his wife's legacy to move the
family to a large house in Somerset with fifty acres of
land which he intended to farm. You had only to look
around you at the wealthy farmers in Crome on market
day, he told his wife and her sister, who came to look
after her and the children after old Honeyman died, to
see that it was a profitable business.

It may have been fifty acres were not enough for his
purpose, or that a man who had been born and bred
in farming would find it easier to make a living at it
than a gentleman who had no notion of how to set
about it, but at the end of every year his enterprise
showed a steady loss and debts began to mount again
forcing him to raise a mortgage on his property. This
however did not prevent him from entertaining on a

lavish scale, and after his wife died Sukey still had to go to her expensive school in Bath, Martha to have her pianoforte and her music lessons, and Charles to have his tutor so that in years to come it was scarcely surprising that the Captain's death left his children with only a hundred apiece after all the debts were paid.

Deborah, whose three thousand was untouched, found a neat little house in Crome to rent for three pounds ten shillings a quarter, and here she had been anxious to give a home to her nephew and nieces had not her brothers persuaded her that Mr. Lingford was more able and certainly had more legal right to be their guardian. For Martha, however, the fear of debt was never absent and recently it had started teasing her in the peace of the Bowery.

How long could she go on there without running into debt herself? The thought had kept her awake at night and as she thought now of Sukey and Charles and the small amount of money they had left in the world she knew that for their sake she should accept her grandfather's offer.

"Very well," she said quietly. "We will move from the Bowery: it is kind of you to offer us a home with you here at Rydd House and I know my brother and sister will appreciate it." She expressed no thanks on her own behalf and although it irritated him he knew that he could not blame her. But because of a promise he had made to Charles on the journey to Portsmouth that he would look after his sisters, he said nothing except that he would send a servant to Mrs. Spry to settle the bill there and to have their luggage fetched.

"Thank you, but I will go myself," Martha said and the following morning she set out in the little cart with

Jonas to say goodbye to Mrs. Spry and the charming little cottage.

The marsh round Rydd House was harsh and bare, the birds that flew over it were mostly gulls. But round the Bowery flowers grew, buttercups and the white heads of the sea-kale, and larks sang in a peaceful heaven. It had been a haven for them all and although she knew she could not afford to stay there she had enjoyed the feeling of independence it had given her.

The price she was asked to pay for her family's new home was an irksome dependence on the uncertain whims of an old man whom she could not forgive for his behaviour to her parents, nor like for himself and while conscious that she would rather scrub floors than accept it for herself, yet she felt too that it might not be too large a price if Sukey and Charles were to be provided for and happy.

Eleven

A few days later Mr. Lingford had occasion to visit Rydd and having walked into the town he noticed that the smiles that usually accompanied the greetings of some of its inhabitants were strangely lacking. One or two scarcely returned his salutation at all, and in fact several, when they saw him coming, crossed the street deliberately to greet somebody else or to find deep interest in a shop window.

He could not understand such coolness from people who had been his friends for many years and presently he made his way up the twitten that led to the forge to find Goliath Pipe. The smith was hammering out a glowing piece of iron on his anvil and the coolness seemed to have spread to him too, because he acknowledged Mr. Lingford's presence by a curt nod and did not stop his hammering for a moment.

The old man walked home in a temper that was far from sweet and sought out Jonas, finding him in the yard polishing harness.

"Has anything happened in Rydd while I've been away?" he asked. "Anything that I should know about and do not?"

"What makes you think that, sir?" asked Jonas, his wits even slower than usual.

"Come, man, stop your rubbing and answer me!" His master was angry. "Why was I so shunned this morning? Why do I appear to have no friends left in the town?"

"Like as not 'tis thought you might hev hed summat to do with the Excise men being round Rydd House while you was gone," Jonas said unwillingly.

"The Excise men? What the devil do you mean? Answer me, or I'll take my crop to you."

After some further hesitation Jonas told him of a night when shots had been fired after smugglers across the marsh. " 'Twas as if the Excise had known as you was away and meant to catch 'em, but they've left us alone all these years, hev the Excise and 'tis queer they was to come those few nights. The house was surrounded by 'em, sir. I saw 'em myself in the moonshine, clear as day, on the watch, and Dury's men jest walked into 'em. 'T'was a wonder they wasn't all cotched and killed. Moon was bright 'nough."

Henry Lingford scowled. "Who put the Excise fellows up to it?" he wanted to know. And then as Jonas did not answer he said slowly, "Surely they don't think I did? And yet—they might I suppose. Do they think that?"

" 'Pears as if some folks do think that way, sir," said

Jonas uncomfortably. "Dury has been saying as you told 'un to use the coach-house here as usual when you was away, but 'twas to be fur the last time, and it was plain by that as you mean the Excise to catch 'em and hev done with 'em fur good an' all. 'Tis said that by doing that no blame could be attached to you, sir."

" 'Tisn't true. I would never have done such a thing. You know that as well as I do, Jonas." But Henry Lingford's anger had evaporated and he looked utterly dismayed.

"Yes, sir." Jonas went back to his rubbing. "All 'same Dury's saying as he'll kill you fur it and things like that. I'd be careful how you go about nights if I was you, sir, and keep close 'til tempers is cooled."

"I'll keep close for nobody. Neither Dury nor anybody else is going to frighten me." But Henry Lingford was worried all the same.

The French *émigrés* were at Meldrum for a month and during that time Sukey translated for them, taught them English and construed their wants into English for the benefit of Lady Connington and her housekeeper. She also played with the little girl Thérèse and walked in the gardens with the new marquis, Jules de Salle.

In the meantime at Rydd House Martha did her best to accommodate herself to her grandfather's moods, keeping out of his way when he appeared to be in a tantrum and ignoring any sudden attack upon herself that could be designed to provoke a quarrel. On evenings when he was in a more gracious mood she played cribbage with him, being careful to allow him to win and paying over the sixpences he won from her with good grace.

She felt that as the old man was giving her and her

family hospitality he must be humoured and that it was her duty to be tolerant, and she concluded that his dislike for herself stemmed from the evening of their arrival when she had shown him the contempt she felt for what she had found at his house.

One evening after a dinner that had been more silent than usual a message was brought to her grandfather that a man wished to see him. When he came back he told her that he had to go out but that he would be back before dark and she must drink her tea without him. He then started off on the walk to the town, carrying a stout ash stick with him.

As he never discussed his business with her nor expected her to show any interest in it, she took the handkerchiefs that she was making for Charles into the great parlour and sat by the window sewing until Ben came in with the candles and she realized that dusk was beginning to creep into the room.

"Has your master returned?" she asked.

"No, miss." She glanced at him quickly and thought he seemed uneasy.

"Do you know where he has gone?" she asked.

"I reckon he went to see summon in the 'arbour, miss."

"In the harbour?" She was surprised and a little of the man's uneasiness touched her too. "But has he gone to see the master of one of the boats there?"

"I'm feared he has, miss." Ben hesitated and then burst out, "The man what brought that message was one of Dury's men. He's an idle, good-fur-nowt, who has only worked for Dury because—" He broke off. "Least said soonest mended," he muttered.

But, of course, like all other honest fishermen in

Rydd the master of the *Turk* was employed in smuggling: she had learned since she came to Rydd that this was nothing to be concerned about.

"Wasn't it Dury's boat, the *Turk*, that brought our French friends to safety?" she asked, puzzled because if it were so then Dury and his crew might be considered to be her grandfather's friends.

"Yes, miss, it were." Ben stood for a moment at the windows peering into the darkness of the lane beyond the garden wall.

"Did you hear what the message was?" she asked.

"As fur as I could hear it seems Dury had some more Frenchies axing of him to meet their friends in the Channel like, and he wanted Mr. Lingford's advice."

"Well, that seems reasonable enough Ben. Why are you uneasy about it?"

"Because I know what is being said in the town about Dury and they last lot of Frenchies. He's no friend of they and he's sworn he'll not fetch another Frenchman not for a thousand pound of good English money."

"Then—why do you think he sent this message?" she asked slowly..

"I reckon it may be a trap, miss, set fur to ketch the master on his way home. It's been said that Dury's sworn to be even with 'un and that one of these dark nights the old gentleman will find 'isself in a ditch with 'is throat cut, like 'is friend the Frenchie. Mind you, miss, Dury was drunk when he said it, so there's no cause to pay much 'eed to 'un. But it do seem odd as he's sent for the master 'stead of coming to see 'un like he allus did do."

"It does indeed." Martha got up and stared out of

the window remembering the rough voice she had heard on the night the *émigrés* arrived. The road to Rydd was open enough where it ran through the marsh, but there was that dark belt of trees, thick enough to hide half a dozen men if they wanted to lay in wait for somebody.

"Is Jonas there?" she asked.

"No, miss. The master give 'im leave to go to the Tenterden fair and 'e won't be back come midnight and then, by my reckoning, dead drunk."

"Then there are only you and me," said Martha.

"You, miss?"

"Yes, Ben, me. Will you please go and harness Placid to the chaise at once? Are there brackets in it for lanterns?"

"Yes, miss."

"Then light the candles in them and set them on either side of the carriage. They will shed enough light on the road to keep us out of the ditch. It is a stormy night and the moon is lost to us at present. By the time you have the carriage ready and Placid in the shafts I shall be at the front gate."

"But Miss Lingford, ma'am, Placid has gone lame and Fidget don't take kindly to the shafts."

"He will have to take kindly to them tonight," she said firmly. "Do as I say, Ben."

"But where be us going, miss?"

"To the harbour, where you are to find your master and bring him away from the *Turk*—or anywhere else," she said in a tone that brooked no argument. She went away upstairs while he fetched the chaise and by the time he brought it round with a restive Fidget starting at shadows she was ready for him, with a mantle thrown over her shoulders and the hat that Drum Connington so much deplored tied on slightly askew.

Ellen Muspratt had met her in the hall and when she explained what she was going to do the housekeeper was horrified.

"Oh, Miss Lingford, dear, you cannot go to the harbour this time of night!" she cried. "Let Ben go by himself. It ain't safe for a young lady to go down there. You might be robbed—or . . ." She broke off.

"I shall have Ben with me," Martha told her soothingly. "And I do not think anybody will attack us." She caught sight of the case of pistols on the table in the parlour and acting on a sudden impulse she took one of Charles's weapons from it.

"Oh, Miss Lingford, dear, you can't take that!" Ellen was shocked to the core. "They nasty old firearms— you cannot fire 'em and neither no more can Ben."

"Neither of us will fire this pistol," Martha said soothingly. "It is not loaded, but it may serve to frighten anybody who attempts to attack us on our way home." She went out to the chaise followed by the protesting housekeeper, and assuaged Ben's equally strong apprehension at seeing the weapon in her hand with the same information, that it was only intended as a safeguard.

"But if we return by the back lane," she added, "there should be little danger. It is dry enough for Fidget, isn't it Ben?" The back lane to Rydd House was sometimes under water.

"Dry as a bone, miss." He hesitated. "Would you like me to take that old blunderbuss what's 'anging in the master's room?"

"Is it loaded, Ben?"

" 'Tis allus kept loaded I reckon."

"And have you ever fired it, Ben?"

"Can't say as I ever hev, miss."

"Then we will leave it behind." He let down the step for her to enter the chaise and she put the pistol beside her on the seat. "Up you get and quickly," she said. "It is getting darker every moment."

He got up into the coachman's seat and touched the horse with the whip, a totally unnecessary encouragement as Fidget never needed persuasion. He bounded forward and they set off at a great pace towards the town.

The harbour was full of boats, the tide going out fast, and the lights from the taverns round about revealed only battened hatches and furled sails. Out at sea the waves were fairly high and the wind was strong, blowing off the water.

The *Turk* was standing a little way out, riding at anchor and there did not seem to be anybody aboard nor any lights showing.

Martha wondered if she had let her fears for her grandfather's safety bring her out on a fool's errand and was at a loss to know what to do next.

"Maybe the master will be in the Mariners' Arms," Ben suggested, with a nod towards the inn from which a great deal of noise and laughter was proceeding.

"Do you think it likely?" Martha glanced at the inn apprehensively. The Mariners' Arms was noted, so Mrs. Spry had told her, for being patronized by the smuggling gentry at night.

Ben replied that seeing as the *Turk* wasn't in harbour it was more than likely that the meeting had been arranged in the inn.

"Then please go and see if my grandfather is there, and if he is, bring him out. Tell him I want him urgently," Martha said, not having the least idea what excuse she should offer the old man if he were there except her fears for his safety.

Ben swung himself down, attached Fidget's reins to a bollard and crossed the quay into the Mariners' Arms, and after a little while spent in semi-sober argument with his master, he returned with Henry Lingford, who had certainly had more drink than was good for him and was accordingly in an extremely belligerent mood. His fury was increased at finding his granddaughter waiting for him in the chaise.

"Who the hell gave you permission to take my chaise out at this time of night?" he demanded. "And with Fidget in the shafts too!"

"Placid is lame" she reminded him. "And I am trying to save you from being found in a ditch tomorrow morning with your throat cut. If I was wrong I beg your pardon, but the man you were invited to meet tonight has been heard to say that he intends to kill you. If you have met him in that—tavern—then the message was a genuine one." She paused but he did not answer, because Dury had not been at the Mariners' Arms and he had waited for two hours or more for him and had got himself drunk in the meantime. She saw him sway and said quickly, "Please to get in, sir. Ben, help your master in and then free Fidget and we will be on our way."

"You cannot give orders to me or to my servants, you young termagant." The old man knocked Ben's helping hand to his side. "And you need not have humoured her either, you damned fool. Do you think

I am not capable of holding my own, old as I am, against a bunch of murdering ruffians—if they exist outside your imagination?"

"Mr. Lingford sir, I've heard things in the town this past week or more and so has Jonas. There's been threats against you, sir, and that man what come with the message fur you tonight would cut his own mother's throat fur sixpence. You'd much better goo along inside the chaise with Miss Lingford. We'll take the back lane to the house. It's quite dry."

"There'll be no back lanes for me, dry or waterlogged." He would not admit that he had seen in the message a peace-offering from Adam Dury and had seized on it eagerly for that reason. But Dury had not been at the Mariners' Arms where he had been told to meet the man, and his old friends there had turned their backs on him and let him drink alone. Which was perhaps why he had drunk more than was good for his wits. "Now you are here," he told Ben, venting his anger on the two people who had come to rescue him from his unpleasant evening, "I will take the reins and drive the chaise back to Rydd House. But not by the back lane. No man living is going to stop me from entering my house by the front door. I do not skulk or cower for anyone." He took off his hat to Martha and bowed unsteadily. "Your servant, Miss Termagant." Unwillingly Ben helped him up to the box and he took up the reins with his servant beside him.

Martha sat back in the chaise and the light from the quay touched the pistol lying on the seat beside her. Old Lingford's scepticism had shaken her: after all he knew these rogues of the harbour as well as Ben, and no doubt he knew exactly the amount of credibility that could be given to them.

Feeling mortified because it was not from any love of interference, nor from any affection for himself that she had gone out that evening, she reproached herself for having listened to a servant's fears as they made their way to the west gate and swore that it was the last time she would attempt to save her grandfather from himself. No doubt he was his own worst enemy.

And then as they reached the belt of trees halfway along the road the clouds parted and the moon came out fitfully, and as the chaise drew level with the trees she thought she could see a shadow move. Looking out of the open window of the chaise it seemed to her then that everything happened at once.

Two men sprang from the trees and barred their way, seizing Fidget's head, while a third man ran round to pull Mr. Lingford to the ground. He would have succeeded too, Ben being more concerned with taking the reins from his hands and trying to control the plunging Fidget, had not Martha put her head out of the window and called to them to desist. "If you do not leave my grandfather alone," she cried, seeing that they took no notice of her, "I have a pistol here and I shall fire!" She took the pistol from the seat and pointed it out of the window at the man who was struggling with the old man and cocked it.

And then, because of fright or her desire to rescue her grandfather or a feeling of helplessness, her finger tightened on the trigger and immediately there was a report that sent her backwards into the carriage. The men fell back, Fidget flew forwards, and Ben had all he could do to stop him from overturning them all in the ditch.

By the time they reached Rydd House he had managed to bring the frightened animal to a halt and as Martha sprang down into the road without waiting for the steps to be lowered she saw that her grandfather was unconscious.

"Is he drunk?" she asked.

"I don't reckon as it's drink 'tirely, miss. His hat is gone and the ruffian what was trying to get 'un down 'it 'im once or twice."

"Stay with him," she said with an anxious glance at the lolling figure on the box. "I will see if Jonas is back and able to come and help you. We must get him inside the house and up to his bed as soon as possible. And if he has been seriously hurt then one of you must take Fidget and go for Dr. Tilling."

The two menservants, Ben and the returned and repentant Jonas, still somewhat fuddled, got the old man upstairs where Martha with the help of Ellen Muspratt discovered that all he had received was a glancing blow over one eye, the hat having saved him from anything worse. Martha bathed it with strips of clean linen supplied by Mrs. Muspratt, and then, instructing Ben to sleep in his master's room that night in case he moved and needed help, she gratefully accepted a hot posset from the housekeeper before retiring to bed herself.

The posset made her sleep, although it did not stop her from dreaming. The man who had attacked her grandfather had shouted at him and she could not think where she had heard the voice before.

It was only when she woke that she knew where it was: it was the voice she had heard in her grandfather's room on the night after the *émigrés* arrived.

Twelve

The news of the attack and of Martha's part in it spread rapidly through Rydd and beyond. At Meldrum Sir William was able to soothe Sukey's fears for her grandfather's safety by assuring her that Dr. Tilling had told him that except for a cut on his head the old gentleman had been unhurt.

He kept to himself the feeling that it was a pity that the old rascal's grand-daughter had interfered.

When Drum suggested to his mother that she should drive over to Rydd House with Sukey to enquire after Mr. Lingford he was met by a flat refusal.

"Sukey is employed with the little girl this morning, and I cannot leave my guests as you know, Drum. It would be most discourteous. And in any event I have no wish to have anything more to do with Miss Lingford

151

or her grandfather. I consider the whole episode to be quite shocking." Thus Lady Connington, her lips pursed, her face grave with disapproval.

"In what way is it shocking, Mamma?" asked Drum, putting up his quizzing glass to watch Sukey walking with Jules de Salle beyond the window, while Thérèse followed them with her nurse.

"Why, for a young lady to go down to Rydd Harbour at night to fetch an old man out of one of those rough inns on the quay was a most indelicate thing for any well-brought-up young female to do. And as if that were not enough, to fire a pistol at the ruffians who attacked them on the way home! My dear Drum, it was the behaviour of a hoyden!"

"It does not occur to you that Miss Lingford exhibited courage and presence of mind?"

"Certainly not. Your sisters would *never* have behaved in such a fashion."

"They would have fainted on the spot, which would have been no help to the old man, who would undoubtedly have been murdered," said Drum ironically.

"You may defend Miss Lingford if you like, Drum, but you must admit that no man could seriously admire a young woman who behaved in that way."

"On the contrary, I would not be surprised if every man in the neighbourhood does not wish to meet Miss Lingford—in fact I have no doubt that she will become the toast of the county."

"Drum! You are not serious? I trust *you* do not find yourself attracted by that young woman?"

"Attracted, no. Interested, yes. I find her stimulating after the proper behaviour of all the young ladies I know. No man could find himself bored in the company of Miss Lingford." He smiled at his mother. "I think I shall ride over myself and find out how they both do. Miss Sukey will be relieved to have news of them at first hand, I am very sure."

Lady Connington wished she could believe that was all that was as the back of his visit. It would be like her only son to reject every well-brought-up young lady in favour of this tempestuous petticoat.

Drum found the old man downstairs, sitting in an armchair by the fire in his little room, in a very bad temper. He replied to his enquiries grumpily and although his head was still bandaged he brushed it aside as being a mere scratch, exaggerated by a parcel of women.

"I hope Dr. Tilling is reassuring?" said Drum.

"He is an old woman himself. He makes me keep this bandage on though there is nothing beneath it. He dressed the wound yesterday with yellow basilicum ointment which it did not need, and I trust he will do no more to it today. His ointment does more harm than good and I shall tell him so."

It was at this moment that the good doctor was shown into the room by Mrs. Muspratt who waited to see if he would require linen or bowls of water, and Drum took his leave, disappointed at not having seen Martha. She was in the hall however, and had evidently been waiting to speak to him.

"Mr. Connington," she said directly, "I am sure you know how to load and unload pistols?"

"I believe I do, Miss Lingford," he drawled, recalling with amusement his mother's opinion of young ladies who showed an unwomanly interest in such matters.

"Then perhaps you will be so obliging as to examine

my brother's pistols for me and tell me which is loaded and which is not, because I do not like keeping loaded weapons in the parlour."

She led him into the great parlour and showed him the case of pistols on a side-table.

"I may presume," he said as he opened it, "that it is one of these that saved your grandfather's life a few days since?"

He saw her colour slightly. "I protest that I did not know it was loaded," she assured him and went on, "I do not know which of us was the more shocked when it went off like that—my grandfather, Ben his servant, poor Fidget, or myself and our attackers. You see, I have never fired a pistol before in my life."

Her eyes were so roundly shocked by what she had done and her face so surprised that his languor left him and he laughed, and the expression on her face changed and softened and she laughed too. She had, he concluded, a most delightful laugh.

"Give them to me," he said. "I will make them safe for you." He took one out of the case and told her it had been fired. "That presumably is the one you used?"

"It must be. I am so thankful that it fell back into the chaise. Had it dropped outside and one of those— men—found it Charles would never have forgiven me. He sets immense store on these pistols."

"They are very fine weapons." He took the loaded one out of the case and unloaded it swiftly, returning the shot to the small leather case that held others. "There, that is safe now," he told her and then as she returned the weapon to its case beside the other her sleeve slipped from her wrist and he gave an exclamation. "Miss Lingford, what have you done to your arm? It is black and blue."

"It is nothing." She adjusted her sleeve quickly. "The pistol kicked—I believe that is the right word for what happened?—It caught my wrist and Dr. Tilling, to whom I showed it when my grandfather was not by, told me I was fortunate not to have broken my arm. It is only bruised, Mr. Connington. I put some of Mrs. Muspratt's green oil on it and the stiffness is going away. Pray do not say anything of it to Sukey."

"I will not mention it." But he took her hand and gently turned back the sleeve to assure himself that it was, as she had said, only a bruise. "It must have been very painful."

"It is nothing." She took her hand away abruptly and changed the subject. "When do your friends leave you for London?"

"Next Wednesday se'enight we think." His eyes were studying her disconcertingly and she turned from him to the hall, reminding him that he must go if he were to reach Meldrum by dinner time.

"We shall expect Sukey home that day then. My grandfather will be pleased: he finds it dull without her." She asked if he would take a letter to her sister for her: she had written it that morning to reassure her on her grandfather's health.

"I shall be delighted to be your postman." He waited while she fetched it and as he rode off with it in his pocket he was impatient with himself for the interest she roused in him. He had never in his life met a young woman so anxious for the welfare of others and so little concerned for herself, and his dislike deepened for the old man who valued her so little.

On his departure Dr. Tilling annoyed Henry Lingford still more by telling him that his grand-daughter was the heroine of the neighbourhood.

"Her name is on everyone's tongue and wherever I go I am questioned about her. Did she really face three men on her own, and did she shoot one of them with your pistol? The three men have already become masked, and will soon increase to half-a-dozen desperate ruffians and the pistols to two, fired by Miss Lingford in succession as she came to your rescue. All the same you must be very proud of her, and grateful too, because she undoubtedly saved your life."

Henry Lingford growled out an inaudible reply, the doctor catching something about busybodies always being ready to pry into other folks' business, before he went on his way.

"I have told Mr. Lingford that no more ointment is necessary," he informed Martha as he met her coming out of the great parlour. He dropped his voice. "And may I ask how that bruise of yours is progressing?"

She showed it to him and laughed about it, and he took his leave, mounting his cob in the yard and riding off to Rydd. She watched him go and looked at her wrist after he had gone as if she were seeing another hand that had held it lightly for a moment, and other fingers that had gently touched the bruise. It was absurd how Drum Connington's touch had upset her: it was Sukey after all who was to win the admiration of a man like Mr. Connington. She wondered if her grandfather had been right when he had said that her sister's stay at Meldrum had been occasioned by his interest and that the French *émigrés* had nothing to do with it.

In his little room while he waited for his dinner old

Henry Lingford sat glowering and cursing his grand-daughter for having overset all the plans he had made when he invited her to bring her brother and sister to make their home with him.

There was Sukey disporting herself at Meldrum, and Charles in Portsmouth: only their termagant of a sister remained and his dislike for her was rapidly becoming an obsession.

All the plans he had for subduing her had come to nothing: it was she who had humiliated him with the protection she had afforded to a drunken old man. According to Jonas some even said that she had entered the Mariners' Arms herself to fetch him home. Humiliation could strike no deeper than that.

Moreover, now that her praises were being sung everywhere, he would have a string of callers, ostensibly to pay their respects to him, but in order to make his grand-daughter's acquaintance and to show their admiration for a young woman who had simply fired one of Charles's pistols out of a carriage window.

Sitting there in his little room nursing his sore head and his grievances his feeling for her grew to hatred, and he planned how he could humiliate her as she had humiliated him. It was not long before Sukey put the answer into his hands.

The first callers to satisfy their curiosity about Miss Lingford were the Racksbys. Sir George's wife and daughters paid a morning call and were entertained by Mr. Lingford until his grand-daughter made a hurried appearance, having hastily substituted an old white morning gown for an equally old brown one. The impression she made on them was disappointing.

Far from being the imperious heroine of a nocturnal adventure, Miss Lingford scarcely opened her mouth and when Lady Racksby invited her to the ball they were planning at Racksby before the French *émigrés* left Meldrum, she replied that she did not dance.

"Not dance?" Leonora and her sister Charlotte looked at each other in amazement. "But I thought every young lady danced?" said the elder Miss Racksby.

"My grand-daughter does not behave as young ladies usually do," remarked Mr. Lingford dryly and they were amused to see Martha flush faintly. They said later when they were going home in the carriage that they did not understand Miss Lingford at all.

"Her sister is so gay and so pretty," said Leonora.

"And her gowns are pretty too, if simple," added her sister. "But Miss Lingford might be the housekeeper. Indeed, when she came into the room I took her for the housekeeper, did you not, Mamma?"

"I do not think she can have a maid to dress her hair," said Lady Racksby.

"No indeed," agreed Leonora. "It was so untidily dressed, with a green ribbon banded in it and tied at the back in a bow that had one end long and the other end short."

"She had not a word to say for herself," added her mother and later on when these criticisms of Miss Lingford were related with much laughter to Sir George over dinner he said that he was not surprised.

"No young lady, however spirited she might be, would induce me to call upon old Henry Lingford," he said. "No doubt she is sharp enough to realize that his bad reputation is known to everybody and she was embarrassed by your visit. I do not wonder that she refused the invitation to your ball. Little Miss Sukey will be much happier without her."

Sukey certainly did not refuse to go to the Racksbys' ball and she enjoyed it enormously, dancing more dances than were quite proper perhaps with the new Marquis de Salle, but his French way of dancing did not come easily to English young ladies although she had spent some time in teaching him the English dances before they set out. Leonora found no fault with his absorption with pretty Sukey: she was glad to observe that Drum Connington, having danced with Sukey once, appeared to think that he had done his duty by her, and danced the next two with herself, then two with her sister, and then two more with herself again. Lady Connington and Lady Racksby watched them smiling, the feathers in their heads nodding approval.

"I understand that you called on Miss Lingford," Lady Connington said. "What was your ladyship's impression of her?"

"I have seldom seen two sisters so unlike as Miss Lingford and her sister," said her ladyship. "We had heard such things about her that I scarcely knew what to expect. But we found nothing more than an ordinary, plain young woman, who sat there not opening her mouth, except to say that she did not dance." She added with a laugh, "Leonora was so witty about her, she kept us all in fits of laughter over dinner that night."

When Leonora tried to be witty about Miss Lingford to Drum Connington, however, he deliberately changed the subject by asking if she had seen much of his sister Fanny, the last time she was in Bath. And however much she tried to come back to Miss Lingford he adroitly steered her remarks back to Bath, until she was sick of that beautiful city and told him frankly that the air did not agree with her, that she never drank the waters, that she found the buildings far too white and glaring for her taste, and Bath society extremely dull.

"It is," he drawled, "a dead bore. But then so many people I find, Miss Racksby, are dead bores, are they not?"

"Miss Lingford—" she began desperately.

"Now that is a young lady," he said imperturbably, "who could never under any circumstances be described as a bore. I notice that she has made such a deep impression on you, for example, that you are eager to talk of nobody else. You must guard against that, Miss Racksby. Young ladies who dwell on one subject to the exclusion of all else might be classed as bores themselves."

She did not reply. They went down the dance in silence and parted at the end of it without speaking again. Drum Connington decided that he would visit the card room for a game of whist.

Fortunately for Martha's peace of mind Miss Racksby's wit kept other callers away from Rydd House, and a few days after the ball the French *émigrés* left Meldrum for London. Lady Connington said goodbye to them with only a half-hearted regret: she was not as sorry as she should have been to see the back of them, as they had a most disruptive influence on the household. The food had not been right for their French stomachs, the rooms were too cold or too draughty, the grounds too wet for them to walk with comfort, while at all times they regaled her with terrible stories of the sufferings of their friends and relatives, which, owing to their bad English and her own lack of French, she found it difficult to understand. It had been a highly exhausting visit and when Sukey suggested that she should return home on the same day she did not persuade her to stay. She felt the sooner she could see Meldrum cleared of its visitors the better.

Old Henry Lingford was delighted to see his younger grand-daughter, telling her that he would soon be himself again now that the sunshine had returned to his house. Martha was happy too, because Sukey was looking so well after her visit, even if she had picked up affectations that she had not had before.

Over dinner she was full of the Racksby ball. "Lady Connington had a *frisseur* to dress our heads," she told them. "And I was glad she did because all the other ladies had their hair dressed—though not powdered, of course, as the Marquise wanted, but when we told her that English powder was mostly made of white flour she did not insist on it. As to the ball I have never seen anything like it before. We went to assemblies at Crome, did we not, Martha? But they were such small dull affairs compared with this. Why, there must have been nearly a hundred people there, and the supper was so good and the greenhouse looked so beautiful. I wish you had been there, but Lady Racksby said you had told her that you did not dance." She gave a little laugh. "I knew what *that* meant, though I did not tell her so!"

"I should hope you did not," said Martha. "As I had no ball-gown I could scarcely have gone in any case, could I? And how was I to get there pray?"

"Oh, Mr. Connington said he would have come for

you in his carriage," rattled on Sukey.

"That would not have been necessary," said her grandfather frowning. "As to your sister's gown, if she wished for one I daresay she would have been able to buy it."

"Thank you, but I did *not* wish for a ball-gown," said Martha.

Certainly Sukey's return to Rydd House had a great effect on Henry Lingford. There was a spell of good weather that July and the lanes smelt of honeysuckle and hay, and Rydd House had a succession of young gentlemen paying morning calls on Mr. Lingford and his pretty grand-daughter. The old man was highly amused by these visitors and commented on them to his elder grand-daughter with his usual coarseness.

"Sukey evidently made an impression on the Conningtons' friends," he mused. "They are sniffing round her like dogs after a bitch in season."

Martha tried to discover some preference for any one of them in Sukey, but her sister treated them all alike, with a light airy nothingness akin to flirtation, learned from the Miss Racksbys which amused her grandfather exceedingly. Even Mr. Algernon Makins, a young man who was a friend of Drum Connington's and reputed to be heir to vast estates and a great fortune, was not singled out for better treatment, and when Martha remarked on the gentleman's splendid turn-out in the lane Sukey said she had not noticed. "He sat there ogling me until I could have boxed his ears," she added.

"He is heir to a title." Having enquired privately from her grandfather about the young man's prospects Martha took her to task gently for her light dismissal of him, because it was for just a wealthy marriage and a position in the world that Sukey had been educated at Miss Miller's superior establishment in Bath, not for the entertainment of a handful of French *émigrés*. "If you married him you would have all the money you could ever want, Sukey, dearest, besides two houses in Scotland, one in Kent and a mansion in London."

"And what would that matter if I did not love him?" demanded Sukey. "If in fact I detested him, as I do. One cannot live in four houses at once. I wish you were more romantic Martha: you think of nothing except what a man has of money and establishments. Why, Leonora said that in her opinion Mr. Makins had as much sense as would go on a sixpence."

"Miss Racksby might have changed her mind had she found that Mr. Makins admired her instead of you," said Martha dryly. After a moment she continued, remembering the society to which her sister had become accustomed at Meldrum, "Penniless young gentlemen can no doubt be charming—much more charming than some wealthy young gentlemen. Their situations are romantic their futures not likely to be dull or predictable. But Sukey, my love, I would not like you to lose your heart to a man without any money—somebody, shall we say, like M. de Salle."

"What makes you mention him?" Sukey flung round at her sister, surprising and dismaying her by her anger. "Has Lady Connington been writing to you complaining of my behaviour with Jules de Salle? She did not approve from the start of my visit because I found his society preferable to that of her precious son, the great Drum Connington. But she may say what she likes, there is nobody to compare with M. de Salle.

He is handsome and charming, and he knows what to say to a woman—"

"I am sure that he does." Martha spoke quietly, her fears now thoroughly roused. "But does he know that you are as penniless as he is?"

"The de Salles are not penniless." Sukey laughed scornfully. "Once this dreadful revolution in France is finished they will go back to France, with all the other French *émigrés*, and they will claim back the estates and money that have been stolen from them. There are very great prospects in front of M. de Salle."

"I wish it were so with all my heart." Martha knew that her grandfather did not believe in any golden future before the French *émigrés*. "Once a mob gets its hands on to a man's possessions it will not lightly let them go," he had told her one day when discussing the French troubles with her. And what would be the use of ruined estates to a French nobleman however aristocratic he might be? "Will you at least promise me one thing, Sukey dearest," she went on persuasively. "Try not to think of M. de Salle too much, and if he should visit us here—or write to you—or anything like that—do not encourage him, my love."

Sukey laughed, her blue eyes wide and innocent. "Now what would be the use of M. de Salle writing a letter to me here at Rydd House?" she asked. "You know what its fate would be. Grandpapa would put it on the fire before I could see it."

"He probably would," agreed Martha, and as Sukey left her with another laugh she thought that perhaps she had been wrong to be anxious and that her sister's fondness for M. de Salle had been no more than another flirtation.

Thirteen

The weather turned warm and on fine mornings Sukey took some of Charles's neckbands into the little arbour overlooking the Hastings road and amused herself by watching the travellers to and from Rydd. They were not a very lively lot: a few loaded London wagons, with their teams of horses, a hired chaise or two, solitary riders whose absence of grooms proclaimed them to be people of no importance and farm-hands driving sheep and cattle to market.

The neckbands did not progress very fast because hidden under the folds of Sukey's skirt were sundry volumes of romantic novels borrowed from the Rydd Library in the High Street, and one morning when Henry Lingford was riding back from the town he happened to look over the wall and saw Sukey in her gazebo and Betsy there with her. The servant had her bonnet and mantle on and he thought that she had just got back from the market before seeing that she had brought a letter for her young mistress.

She was standing beside her while she read it and as neither had eyes for anything but the letter in Sukey's hands old Lingford was able to hand over Placid to Jonas in the stables and make a leisurely way to the little arbour unnoticed.

Sukey was now alone and the letter was being read again with deep delight, and when he spoke she gave a great start and tried to hide it under Charles's neck-bands.

"May I know the name of your correspondent, my love?" he said mildly.

"My—Oh, you mean my letter? It is from an old school-friend, Grandpapa."

"You are not a good liar, my dear." He sat himself down beside her. "Let me see if I can guess the name of the school-friend. She must be a young lady of very strange character if her letters have to be fetched secretly by your servant from some prearranged address in town. Any young lady who had been a school-friend of yours at that superior establishment in Bath would surely have directed her letters to you here at my house? But what if the writer of that letter were not a young lady at all—but rather a young gentleman—a lover, shall we call him? Then indeed I am the more puzzled, because if he were a gentleman like Mr. Drum Connington or his friend Mr. Makins, he would come courting you openly and there would be no need for secrecy either. So who can he be? One must conclude that your correspondent is somebody of whom you fancy your family would not approve. In short it may be Jules de Salle, the Frenchman. Have I guessed right, Sukey?"

"Yes." Her face which had become more and more downcast while he was speaking now appeared almost despairing. "Before he left Meldrum he asked if he could write to me and I said that he could. But I told him not to address his letters here because"—she stopped, glancing at him timidly.

"You were afraid I would burn them?" he asked smiling.

"I was not afraid of *you*!" She slipped her hand into his. "I was afraid of Martha. I dare not let her see his letters so I asked him to address them to "Miss S." in the care of Mrs. Spry at the Bowery. Martha has told me since I have been home that I must not think of him seriously because he has no money, but in this last letter he asks me to marry him, and how can I help thinking of him when I love him to distraction? I know Martha will not let me marry him, and if she does not I will never marry anyone else. And please do not tell her, Grandpapa, because if you do everything will be lost and my heart will break." And she put her face into her hands and burst into tears.

"Come now, there is nothing to break hearts over, so let me hear no more of that nonsense, little Sukey!" Her grandfather put his arm round her and drew her head on to his shoulder and continued smoothly, "I see no reason why Martha should know anything about it. She will not hear of it from me, although there is nothing she can do to prevent your marriage to de Salle if I give my consent. You are under age and according to law I am your natural guardian, not your sister. If I give my consent to your marriage with a chimney sweep she cannot stop it. But we do not want unpleasantness and quarrels, and neither do we want to stir our termagant to militancy. I suggest therefore that you write to M. de Salle and request him to write to me, as your guardian, for my formal consent to your marriage." He reflected that in this way he could assure himself of the young man's intentions towards his grand-daughter. He did not trust Frenchmen, although he had been agreeably impressed with Jules while he was at Rydd House. "You may tell him also that I am not unprepared to provide you with an income after you marry, and that Rydd House will be your home and the home of your husband until he can find you another. But in the meantime he is not to mention it to anybody. The whole affair is to be a secret between you and me and M. de Salle."

Her tears dried like magic. She threw her arms round him and kissed him. "Oh, how good and kind you are!" she cried. "No girl in the world could have found a better grandfather—nor one so dearly loved!"

He returned her kiss smiling, and told her that when her letter was ready for Jules she was to bring it to him herself without her sister's knowledge and he would take it to the post. And as he left her to her love-letter he reflected with satisfaction that Sukey had provided him with a weapon to humiliate his elder grand-daughter in a way he had never dreamed possible. If Sukey married her French marquis and brought him back with her to Rydd House then she would be mistress there and her elder sister would be nothing.

He would settle one thousand pounds a year on Sukey and he would tell her that if she wished to spare a trifle of pin-money now and then for her sister he would raise no objection.

The humiliation of Miss Lingford, who had always held the purse-strings for her family, would then be complete.

It all pleased the old wretch a good deal and he was in an excellent humour for the rest of the day.

One day during the following week a letter was fetched from Rydd for Mr. Lindford, and instead of putting it on the fire he took it to his little room where Sukey joined him later. She had fallen into the habit of sitting with him there after breakfast while she read the morning's newspapers to him, Martha being occupied with the housekeeper.

This time she read the letter to him, as it was in French, and the contents were so acceptable to them both that they had a good laugh about it and she went about the house singing all day and so cheerful that her sister concluded she had finally put the captivating Frenchman out of her mind.

The next day Mr. Lingford told them that he would be setting out for London that morning and would not be returning for a week or two as he had affairs to discuss with his man of business there.

One of the George chaises came to fetch him at eleven o'clock to take him to Tonbridge and after he had gone the girls went into the great parlour where Sukey played on the harpsichord, which was sadly out of tune through lack of use.

"I wish my grandfather had a pianoforte," sighed Sukey. "They had a beautiful new one at Meldrum."

"You must ask your grandfather to buy you one,"

Martha said drily. "He does not seem able to refuse anything you ask him."

Sukey looked at her quickly and blushed. Her conscience accused her of treachery to the elder sister who had looked after her and loved her for so many years, but she was soon able to stifle it with the thought that it was her happiness that was at stake and she was not going to allow Martha to ruin it.

At the end of the week Mr. Lingford returned with an invitation from his only surviving sister, the Dowager Countess of Wray, for Sukey to visit her for a few weeks.

"I had not seen Amelia for years," Mr. Lingford told the two girls. "And at first she refused to see me. But I had written her a letter begging her to let bygones be bygones, and telling her that my grandchildren were now making their home with me, and I waited in the anteroom until she admitted me to her drawing-room. And when I told her how pretty Sukey was she quite relented and suggested that she should visit her. I have promised to take the little madam to her next week."

He had brought back with him ten yards of white muslin for a new gown for Sukey and as Martha admired it with her sister Sukey said in rather a shame-faced fashion that she wished he had brought another ten yards for Martha.

"I don't need new gowns, dearest," Martha said smiling. "But now that our great-aunt is going to introduce you into society this will make a fine new ballgown for you. It needs some lace to trim it but I daresay the blue sash we bought in Bath may do as well."

When Henry Lingford heard that they needed lace he took Sukey up to his dressing-room and told her to fetch down a rosewood box from the top shelf of the wardrobe, and when she opened it there were lengths of French lace inside.

"Valenciennes, I believe," he said, dismissing her with it to her sister and Betsy. "It cannot compare with Irish Limerick or Devon Honiton, but it may be fine enough for your purpose child."

It was certainly fine enough and Martha and Betsy spent happy hours over the new gown, fitting the bodice to Sukey's slender figure, fashioning elbow-length sleeves with lace falling from them, and gathered lace as a loose drapery round the lwo-cut bosom. When it was done Sukey showed herself in it to her grandfather and then it was hung in the closet in her room with blue satin slippers and French gloves bought in Rydd. It was the last thing to be packed in the portmanteau that was to accompany Sukey and Betsy to London.

Martha was up early to see that her sister had some breakfast before she left and she was a little surprised by the warmth of the embrace that Sukey gave her before she followed their grandfather into the chaise, and she thought she saw a hint of tears in Sukey's eyes as she kissed her goodbye. Then the old man called her impatiently and off they went, Ben riding beside them with Betsy behind.

Four days later Henry Lingford returned with his servant, arriving in time for dinner at three o'clock, having travelled through the night to Tonbridge.

"How is Sukey enjoying London?" asked Martha as he joined her in the great parlour to wait for their meal. "I hope my great-aunt approves of her?"

"It does not matter if she approves or not," said her

grandfather. "Sukey was only in her house for one night."

"One night?" Martha stared. "But I thought she was to visit her?" And then as he did not reply, "Where is Sukey, sir?"

"With her husband, no doubt." His expression was gloatingly triumphant. "Your sister was married yesterday morning in London. I was with her and was one of the witnesses."

"Married? Sukey?" She stood as if turned to stone and after a glance at her face the gloating left him and he became slightly apprehensive. "To whom has she been married?" she asked slowly. "Or am I not to know his name?"

"She has married Jules de Salle," he said truculently. "She is now Mme. la Marquise. At least you will approve of that one hopes."

"And will the fact of being Mme. la Marquise feed her or clothe her or find a roof for her head?" Martha walked to the open window and stood there for a moment or two with her back to him, hoping that she would not faint. "When Sukey and I discussed M. de Salle a little while ago I told her that my only objection to him as her husband would be his lack of income, as she herself had no means of her own."

"As to that," he said carelessly, "I saw my man of business while I was in London and I have made a will in which I leave all my possessions, including this house, to Sukey and Charles. In addition I have told M. de Salle that he is to regard Rydd House as his home until he is able to provide his wife with another, and that I intend to settle on Sukey the sum of one thousand pounds a year." He glanced at the motionless figure in the window. "Well? What have you to say to that?"

She was silent for a long moment and then she said as quietly as before, "Why, I can only thank you, sir, for your generosity to Sukey and to my brother. It is more than I dared hope, and I am very much obliged."

"I have told Sukey to allow you pin-money," he went on, angry because he was still speaking to her back and it told him nothing. "So that you will not be penniless."

This final stab struck home but not in the way he had anticipated. She turned from the window, all feeling of faintness gone, her head up, her eyes as cold as ice. "Your generosity overwhelms me, sir," she said. "You have thought of everything." Everything that could hurt and wound and humiliate her, and Sukey had been persuaded—or bribed with one thousand pounds a year —to help him. That was the deepest the most wounding stab of all. She saw Ellen standing in the doorway and wondered how much she had heard. "Yes, Ellen? Is dinner served? Then let us go into the dining-parlour and eat it."

She led the way into the dining-parlour and sat opposite him at the long table there, with the derisive eyes of the portraits upon them, and if the peas and bacon, the couple of ducks roasted, and the gooseberry pie were attacked with relish by him and by her with no appetite at all, it went unnoticed by her grandfather.

After the meal she stayed with him in the parlour until tea was brought in, refusing to discuss her sister's marriage and keeping conversation coldly to local matters: how the pigeons needed shooting as they were getting the peas, and how the brown thread stockings to be worn under his riding boots that she had bought for him in Rydd had cost six shillings, which she considered to be dear. She avoided all reference to Sukey until tea came, after which she excused herself saying that she must write to Charles to tell him of his sister's marriage. And then she said good night and the door closed behind her.

The scenes that Henry Lingford had foreseen with so much relish, and the feeling of having got the better of her at last had not materialized. It was he who felt defeated as he sat alone in his little room after a supper which she had not shared. She was such a strange young woman, he thought angrily. Where one anticipated tantrums and fury she had not played the termagant at all, and had behaved with such a cold and contemptuous restraint that it made him feel ashamed of the part he had played in the whole business.

He did not feel any better the following morning when she met him at breakfast at ten o'clock with a cool discussion of the coffee. Was it hot enough and the correct strength for his taste? Her attention to his welfare and tastes were so detached however that he felt as if she were his housekeeper instead of Ellen Muspratt.

During the days that followed she was able to keep up this façade of restraint before him, although her sleepless nights and agony of mind over Sukey's behaviour gradually built up a feeling of helplessness and fury that had to find an outlet somewhere, if she were not to betray herself to the old man and show him how much he had triumphed. One morning after a breakfast during which she felt she could endure his studied taunts no longer, she made the excuse that she wished to tidy Sukey's gazebo before she returned, and finding an old pocket knife belonging to her brother she went out to where she could be sure of being safe from prying eyes and began to cut away the brambles and ivy that covered the entrance to the little arbour, finding satisfaction in the energy and fury that could be expended on it.

It so happened however that Drum Connington rode over that morning from Meldrum to offer Miss Lingford his own and his parents' felicitations on Sukey's marriage. He had been in London at the time and had been applied to by his friend Jules to be one of the witnesses there. Miss Lingford's absence had puzzled him and it puzzled him still: he did not believe the excuse that Miss Sukey had given him for it.

As he approached Rydd House he glanced over the wall and saw a young woman in a patched morning gown cutting furiously at the creepers that overhung the small gazebo there. She did not hear his approach and dismounting he handed his horse over to his groom telling the man to walk the horses to the trough in Mr. Lingford's yard and water them there, and pushing open the gate he made his way to the gazebo.

When he said good morning Martha whirled about, her face scarlet and her eyes dark with fury. It was obvious that Miss Lingford was letting forth several inner demons on the unlucky creepers.

"Good morning, Mr. Connington," she said without any attempt at civility and still slashing away with the knife. "My grandfather is in the house."

"I did not come to call on your grandfather," he said mildly. "I came to visit you. And you have scratched your hand. It is bleeding badly."

She looked about her for a cobweb and clapped it on to the cut. "Why have you come to see me?" she demanded.

A termagant indeed—or rather, a most tempestuous petticoat. He said, smiling, "I came to felicitate you on your sister's marriage."

"Then had you not better wait until she returns and offer them to her instead? Please go, Mr. Connington. I am in no fit state to receive visitors this morning."

He could see that she was shaking and he was suddenly deeply concerned for her. "Jules asked me to be one of the witnesses at the ceremony," he said gently, "and as you were not there to be with your sister, I was afraid that you might have been ill."

"I am never ill," she said fiercely.

"But I cannot believe that you stayed away because you disapproved of the marriage," he said, his voice betraying doubt and disappointment and she whirled round on him more furiously than before.

"Is that what they said about me?" she demanded. "That I was not at Sukey's wedding because I did not approve of it?"

"Your sister gave me that impression—" He broke off, not willing to sow seeds of discord between them.

"It is an excuse that will serve as well as another, I suppose." She put up her chin. "I can see your horses on the other side of this wall, Mr. Connington. They look impatient. You will oblige me by joining them."

"Something has happened to hurt you," he persisted. "And to anger you. Will you not tell me what it is—as your friend and one whom you can trust?"

"I have no friends," she said bitterly. "And nobody

whom I can trust." And she returned to her slashing of the creepers so determinedly that he could stay no longer.

He turned towards the gate uncertain and anxious and then determined to make one more attempt at gaining her confidence he returned to the arbour. But as he came within a few feet of it he heard muffled sobbing and glancing inside he saw the usually controlled Miss Lingford crumpled up on the seat there, her head bent on her arms which rested on its dilapidated back and her whole body shaken by the force of her weeping.

She had dismissed him so determinedly that he felt he could do nothing without making matters worse, and happening to see Ellen Muspratt come from the direction of the kitchen garden with a bunch of herbs in her hands he went towards her hurriedly.

"Are you the housekeeper?" he asked.

"Why yes, sir." She was a pleasant woman, if a plain one, and she looked capable and kind.

"Then go at once to your mistress. She is in the arbour by the wall there and she is—not herself."

She ran forward to the gazebo and he saw her drop the herbs and heard her voice. "My poor dear, do not break your heart like this—pray don't. Miss Sukey has shown herself to be not worth all the love you gave her and she is not worth one of your tears neither. Nor is that old rascal within, who planned it all—"

Drum had heard enough. He let himself out of the gate and rode off furiously to Meldrum, wondering what devilment old Lingford had been at that could have reduced his tempestuous petticoat to tears.

After a time Martha composed herself and refused

the housekeeper's suggestion that she should go to her room and have dinner sent to her there. She had no wish to delight her grandfather by showing him how much he had hurt her and she said so.

"He hates me with his whole heart," she said.

" 'Tis because you're the living image of your father," Mrs. Muspratt told her. "Mr. Vincent was the only one left out of eight—the other children all died in infancy. Mr. Lingford had set his mind on him marrying the daughter of an old friend in Yorkshire, and your father did not object until he met your mother and fell in love with her. He married her in spite of everything your grandfather could say and Mr. Lingford being a violent-tempered man, never forgave him. You are the only one of Mr. Vincent's children who favours him, and every time Mr. Lingford looks at you and sees you smile he must see his son again and his conscience will not let him rest. So he tries to punish that dead son by teasing and vexing you."

"I think I can understand that." Her tears were dry now and her face had assumed its usual calm expression. "Thank you for telling me, Ellen. I shall know now what to do."

She went indoors and changed into her one best gown for dinner, and when she came down to the meal there were no traces of tears on her face and she was as calm and cool as before.

"Drum Connington's horses were in the yard," said the old man trying to penetrate that calm. "He did not call on me."

"No. He was passing and saw me in the gazebo and stopped to felicitate me on Sukey's wedding. It appears that he was there." Not a muscle of her face betrayed the slightest feeling.

"I daresay he is pleased about it," said her grandfather maliciously.

"I daresay he is," she agreed. "M. de Salle is a friend of his, is he not?"

In the days that followed her calm remained unbroken: it seemed as if she had armed herself against him and the old man thought, "You wait, my lady. When Sukey is home and mistress of this house it will be a very different matter."

Fourteen

Nothing that old Henry Lingford could say during the next few days could provoke his elder grand-daughter. She saw to the preparation of rooms for Sukey and her husband and discussed them with him pleasantly, meeting any jibes he might think to direct towards herself with either a lifted brow or a faint smile, as if he were an ill-mannered child.

A large bedroom on the first floor was set aside for the newly married couple, with a dressing-room for Jules and a sitting room for Sukey. The furniture was old-fashioned but when it had been polished and the curtains replaced by some of crimson damask that Ellen had come upon in an old chest in one of the attics, the rooms looked well enough.

"No doubt," Martha told Ellen as they admired the

freshly hung curtains, "Mme. de Salle will make her own alterations when she returns."

Ellen was too good a servant to comment on the situation or to offer any further sympathy to Miss Lingford but she could not help wondering what fresh indignities would be heaped upon her when the happy couple returned. But apart from that one fit of tears Miss Lingford did not show her feelings: she was true to her class there, Ellen thought. The gentry did not show their feelings. Why, there were tales going about of French aristocrats like M. de Salle who had gone to their deaths over there as proudly as if they were going to a Court ball. In the days before the younger sister came home with her French husband Miss Lingford constantly reminded Mrs. Muspratt of those stories by her calm acceptance of the situation and her lack of emotion. If Ellen had not admired her for it she must have been worried.

A letter from the new Mme. de Salle did nothing to shake that calm: Martha did not comment on its contents but merely made sure that Mrs. Muspratt remembered the day when they could be expected home. She read the letter with a control that her grandfather thought must be forced, but in this he was wrong. She read it with no feelings at all.

It was full of excuses, of "dearest, dearest Martha's", of protestations of Sukey's love for her sister, before going on to rapturous praises of her "beloved husband" and how much he was looking forward to becoming better acquainted with her own Martha. If Sukey had copied out a page from the novel she happened to be reading at that moment it might have affected her sister more.

She put the letter away and on the day before the couple were expected at Rydd House she asked if she might have the little cart to drive into Rydd as she had to visit one of the warehouses there for her sister. Ben took her in the little cart and she executed a couple of errands of her own before she visited the warehouse and then she came home to answer Sukey's letter and to write one to Charles before dinner.

The letter to her brother informed him that she had deposited one hundred pounds with Mr. Capstick the banker in Rydd, and he had promised to see that it would earn interest for him until he was made a lieutenant. As there must be some years to go before then, she added, she felt it might increase in value to some small extent. She then informed him that she would be leaving Rydd the following day and would write to him again when her plans were settled, and remained his affectionate sister, M. Lingford. And as usual, when writing to Charles, she enclosed the fee for the letter under the seal.

She wrote on much the same lines to Sukey, keeping to business matters and telling her that she had deposited a further hundred pounds in her married name with Mr. Capstick's bank. She added that as three hundred pounds had remained to them after their father's death, she had now accounted for their share of the money to Charles and to herself.

The keys to the store-cupboard and the linen-room are in the drawer of the escritoire in your sitting-room as you will now be mistress of your grandfather's house. Your grandfather needs some new shirts, she went on, but Betsy will cut them out for you. You are a good needlewoman and I know you will experience no difficulty with the neck and wrist bands. I am sorry you

*did not think to take me into your confidence over
your marriage: I did not dream that I was such a
dragon. By the time you arrive however that dragon
will have left Rydd House to harmony and to you.
With good wishes for your health and happiness and
compliments to your husband. Yours sincerely, M.
Lingford.*

Having settled these matters and with her mind at
rest she pulled out a small trunk from its corner, glad
that it had not been consigned to one of the attics when
they arrived there, and began to pack in it the few
clothes that she possessed and the even scarcer trea-
sures from her old home—a book of poems, her
mother's prayerbook, a miniature of her father—not
welcome at Rydd House—and the old cribbage board
at which she and her father and her brother and sister
had played so many games in the past. It was queer,
she thought, clasping the old board in her arms, tears
for the first time pressing at the back of her eyes, how
inanimate objects could move one so much more than
human contact at times like these.

When the trunk was packed and ready she sent for
Ellen and told the housekeeper as calmly and rationally
as she had talked and acted since that morning in the
arbour, that she was leaving Rydd the following day.

"I have ordered a chaise from the George and it is
to be here, in the back lane, at six in the morning," she
said. "I would be obliged if you will tell Ben to take
my trunk down the side stairs and out to the lane at that
hour."

"You are going away on a visit, miss?" Ellen was
glad to think that this would be the case.

"No, I am leaving Rydd House for good." She was

touched by Ellen's distressed face. "I know you will work as well for my sister as you have worked for me."

"But—where are you going, miss?"

"I shall go to London first, but after that I have made no plans. And, Ellen," she added as the woman turned to leave the room, "please to say nothing to my grand-father or to the other servants. Nobody is to be a party to this but Ben and you. I do not wish your master to know of my departure until after I have gone." She took Mrs. Muspratt's hand and put a guinea into it. "Look after my sister for me, Ellen dear, and give my love to Betsy, and thank you for all you have done for me. I shall not forget it—or you."

"But—will you not say goodbye to the master before you go, miss?" Ellen was plainly worried over this side of the matter and Martha smiled faintly.

"Once Mme. de Salle is home he will not even know that I am gone."

Before she went to bed that night, however, she stayed for a moment longer than usual beside her grandfather's chair.

"Well, what is it?" he demanded, looking up with a frown. "Do you need more money?"

"On the contrary," she said, "I am returning some to you." She put the purse that he had given her at the Bowery on to the table beside him. "That is the rest of the money you gave me. I spent a little of it on Charles's clothes and the new shoes he had before he went to Portsmouth. Thank you, sir, for your kindness in taking Sukey and Charles off my hands. I am truly grateful for it. Good night. I hope you sleep well." And then she was gone.

He sat for some time frowning at the purse on the

table and wondering what she meant, and only discovered it the next morning when Jonas had the unwelcome task of breaking the news to his master that his elder grand-daughter had left the house. He could tell him no more except that she had said that her destination was London.

It seemed a vague address for a young lady travelling alone. "I daresay she had gone to that damned attorney uncle of hers," growled Henry Lingford, disconcerted and angry. "If she thinks she can have any legal claim on me she is mistaken. I reckon it is that she's after. I shall be having another letter from the rascal soon, and when it comes it will go on the fire."

But no letter came from either of Martha's uncles, nor from Martha herself. It seemed that he had finally driven her out of his life, and her grandfather could find no pleasure in the thought. With nobody to pick a quarrel with and nobody to jibe at the zest had gone out of life and he felt suddenly very old.

Two days after Sukey returned to Rydd House with her husband, Drum Connington had an urgent message from the captain of the *Snipe*, asking him to see him at once.

Drum rode in and made his way to the harbour, where the Revenue cutter was at anchor, and Harry Redfern took him below to his cabin where a small leather trunk of foreign make was standing on the table under the light from the bull's-eye in the roof.

"Do you recognize this?" he asked.

Drum shook his head. "Never seen it in m'life."

"Then do you think young de Salle would recognize it? I am pretty sure that it held his father's money."

"You mean you have found old de Salle's murderer?" asked his friend eagerly.

"I believe I have." Harry rubbed his hands. "Like most criminals he has been so careless that he might as well have shouted it from the castle ramparts."

"A local man eh? Can we get hold of the fellow?"

"His boat is in harbour at this moment," said Harry, and added deliberately, "The *Turk*."

"The *Turk*!" The eagerness in Mr. Connington's face was suddenly replaced by dismay, although he knew he had been expecting something like this ever since he went out on the boat to meet de Salle's family. "You mean Adam Dury is the man?"

"Yes. As I said just now he is careless. He took a thousand pounds worth of louis d'or to a silversmith in Tenterden, where he is well known, and asked him to change it for English gold. He then took this leather box, in which the money was packed, to a leather seller in the High Street there, and he knew him too, very well. Both these men will come forward to give evidence at the trial."

"The trial? Yes, I suppose there will be a trial." Drum spoke slowly, his eyes on the leather box.

"I thought you would be pleased," protested Harry, disappointed. "What is wrong? Why should a murderer not be tried and hanged, be his victim English or French?"

"The nationality of the man he killed has nothing to do with it," said Drum. "If he is brought before the magistrates they will have no choice but to commit him to the next Assizes."

"Or an improvised court here in Rydd," said Harry.

"A court in Rydd or elsewhere makes no odds."

Drum moved his shoulders impatiently. "If it comes to a trial anywhere, Harry, there's going to be the devil to pay. The man is a rat, and like a rat when cornered he will do his utmost to drag others down with him."

"Others?" Harry frowned. "What others, Drum?"

Drum Connington did not answer at once and then he asked abruptly: "How many people in Rydd know that the *Turk* is owned by old Lingford? She *is* owned by him, isn't she?"

"So I believe."

"And has he or has he not taken a share of every cargo over the past ten years?"

"Aye, he has done that," agreed Harry and his face showed now that he was beginning to see the drift of his friend's remarks. "But nobody will ever believe that he had a hand in de Salle's murder."

"Nor that he did not take a share of de Salle's money?"

"That of course one cannot say."

The two young men were silent, considering the matter, and then Drum said unhappily: "Lingford's younger grand-daughter was recently married to Jules de Salle, and my father tells me that the old man has offered the young people a home with him at Rydd House and that he has settled one thousand pounds a year on his grand-daughter. That might be regarded in some quarters as conscience money, Harry."

"But only if it should all come out at Dury's trial, Drum. And first we must have young de Salle's word for it that this box was the one in which his father's money was carried: it is the only thing that will hang Dury. Damme, the fellow's a murderer: he deserves to hang."

"I do not dispute that, but at a public trial we may find young de Salle's old relative by marriage on trial too, and what will be the position then? May not the new marquis be left with doubts in his mind for the rest of his life? He will never be sure that the grandfather of his wife had no part in his father's murder, or that it was because of his share in the French gold that he was so ready to give his grand-daughter a home and an income. The arrest and trial of Adam Dury could pose problems indeed."

"Yet we cannot let the man go free."

"No, that is very true." Again silence fell in the cabin as they considered what should be done and then Harry said:

"I have it! Supposing I were to shadow the *Turk* in the *Snipe* and find an excuse to sink her?"

"An excellent way of disposing of Dury, but it would dispose of more lives than his."

"You may be sure his crew had their share of the money and one could never prevail on them to give evidence against him. No man is going to put his own head in a noose."

Mr. Connington drummed impatiently with his fingers on the table and then he said, "Look, Harry, let me deal with Dury. I may be able to put the fear of God into him so that he leaves this part of the coast and never comes back. If he should refuse to listen then I give you leave to blow the *Turk* out of the water."

"Very well." Harry was plainly uneasy. "Take care what you are at, Drum. He is a dangerous man."

"I know. I am prepared for it. And give me this leather box. I will see if I can persuade Jules to recognize it without telling him the whole truth."

Old Amos was sitting on the quay as was usual on a warm day and Drum stopped beside him to ask if he knew where he could find the master of the *Turk*.

"He was going to see Goliath Pipe," said Amos, screwing up his eyes against the sun. "Leastways that's where he said he was going."

"When will he be back?"

"Don't rightly know, sir. He might be back any-when."

"I will see if I can find him." Drum stared for a moment at the *Turk* riding daintily on the dancing water of that summer day and then he went back to the George to leave the leather box with his groom before going on to the forge. As he entered the twitten leading to it he saw his quarry approaching him.

"Good morning, Dury." He stopped and the other was forced to stop too. For height and breadth of shoulder the men were evenly matched and the twitten was narrow. "A word with you, please."

"Well?" The red-haired man stared him up and down insolently. "What do you want with me, my fine young coxcomb?"

"Only this." There was no hint of a coxcomb in Drum's voice nor in the eyes that held his. "Go back to the harbour at once and take the *Turk* out and do not return because if you do you may find yourself in so thick a fog that you will only be able to see a hangman's noose at the end of it."

"Why—you." A knife came out like a flash and as quickly a hand fastened on to Dury's wrist, gripping it so that the weapon fell with a clatter to the cobbles. Mr. Connington had not controlled teams of spirited horses for nothing.

"Do not be a fool," he said roughly. "Do as I tell you and take your boat away from Rydd and the Kent and Sussex coasts. There are folk in Tenterden who know you and who will give evidence in front of a judge and jury that you changed a quantity of French gold there lately, and that you also sold the leather box that contained it. So take the *Turk*, Dury, and get gone out of Rydd because if you do not I swear I'll see that you hang."

He dropped the man's wrist and walked on and collected his horse and rode on to Rydd House with the leather box strapped to his groom's saddle.

Ben told him that M. and Mme. de Salle were not yet astir but that his master was in his room beyond the dining-parlour.

"It is your master that I have come to see." Drum followed the man into the little room and almost filled it with his height and returned the old man's greeting shortly.

"I suppose your father sent you," said old Lingford disagreeably, "to congratulate your young friend on his marriage."

"He did not send me," Drum said, his drawl pronounced. "And if he knew the truth, Mr. Lingford, I do not think my father would consider such a marriage to be a matter of congratulations for Jules."

"Why, you young puppy!" Old Lingford half rose to his feet. "Do you think you can walk into my house and insult me to my face? I'll show you how I can deal with that, old as I am. I have servants to show you to the door."

"I have come to tell you," said Drum, taking no more notice of his wrath than the buzzing of a fly on the window-panes, "that I believe the murderer of Jules's father has been found."

The fury left Henry Lingford and he subsided in his chair. "Well I am happy to hear it," he said in a quieter tone. "Who is the man?"

"Adam Dury." Drum spoke the name deliberately, watching the incredulity in his face change to fear.

"I'll not believe it," he muttered.

"Yet Dury was stupid enough to change a number of louis d'or at a silversmith's in Tenterden, where he was well known, greed I imagine being the reason: he was likely to get more if he went to somebody who knew him. For the same reason he sold the leather box that had contained the money to a leather seller who knew him. That box is now in my possession: it is an unusual design, finely wrought in Spanish leather. I do not think that Jules will have any difficulty in recognizing it, and no doubt if he identifies it Dury could hang." He removed his eyes from the old man and examined his nails with some care. "I find myself in a quandary, all the same, Mr. Lingford. If I tell my father he will insist on the man Dury being arrested and brought to trial, and Dury, when captured will act like the animal he is. He will twist this way and that, dragging others into the net with him. I do not care, Mr. Lingford, if you are caught in that net, but I do care if members of your family, and the de Salles, who have been through enough in all conscience, should be caught up in it too. So I have advised Dury to leave Rydd with the *Turk* and not to return. I think we shall not have to wait long for his confession."

"Confession? You are speaking in riddles, sir."

"What I mean is that if he follows my advice and

takes the *Turk* out today and does not return he will have confessed to his guilt. But if on the other hand he stays, which I earnestly hope he will not do, then he will have refused to confess. If you have said any prayers lately, Mr. Lingford, I would advise you to pray now that he will go." He drew on his gloves and turned to the door. "I wish you joy of your new grandson, sir. I feel sure he will appreciate everything that you feel you must do for him and his family."

Jules was waiting for him in the hall and greeted him with delight. "We witness your arrival, my dear Drom, from our window and Sukey, she is not dress'. So I 'urry myself to shake your 'and. You will stay to dinner, yes?"

"Unhappily no." Drum put his hand on the young man's shoulder. "You are happy, Jules?"

"In paradise, *mon cher*. Sukey is an angel."

"Long may your paradise last then, my friend. But I am here on a somewhat distressing errand and I need your help. I would spare you if I could."

"It is news of my father?"

"Partly. Come to the gate with me and tell me, my dear Jules, if you are able to recognize a certain leather box."

Jules needed only one glance at the box strapped to the groom's saddle. "It is the box that held my father's money," he said. "Where is it found?"

"In a leather shop in Tenterden. The man had it from—an English seaman, I am ashamed to say."

"But it is as I fear and as you fear too, Drom, though you are too kind to say it to me and my family. My father, having missed the *Turk* in the fog was found by another who rob and kill 'im. That is so, is it not, my dear Drom?"

"I am afraid something like that did happen, Jules." After a moment Drum added, "With your permission I will keep the box in case we arrest the man. It will be needed as evidence against him."

"He is not found then?"

"Not yet I am afraid. In fact, he may never be caught."

"What of it?" Jules shrugged his shoulders. "If he is caught and hanged, it will not bring my father back to life."

Drum was relieved. He had feared an emotional scene with the young Frenchman, and as he did not seem to be too distressed he changed the subject by asking him how he approved of his new sister.

"My new sister?" For a moment he was puzzled and then he smiled. "Oh, you mean Miss Marta. As I have not seen 'er since we arrive I cannot tell you if I approve of 'er or disapprove."

"Not seen her?" Drum was startled. "Is she ill?"

"I do not suppose so. I do not know. You will understand, *mon cher* Drom, that she leaves Rydd 'Ouse on the morning that we arrive. Very early I am told. Sukey is very angry, but as I say Marta shows good sense. It is not good to 'ave two mistresses in one 'ouse'old."

"But—where has she gone?" Drum tried to keep the dismay out of his voice.

Jules replied with another shrug. "Some say to London, some say Somerset. Nobody can be sure, except that she is not coming back."

Fifteen

On his way home Mr. Connington stopped at the George Inn yard and found the post-boy who had driven Miss Lingford to Tonbridge. He could only tell him, however, that she was bound for London and with that he was far from content.

He rode back to Meldrum in a mood that was not happy: haymaking was going on in the fields and it should have reminded him that his own clover crop in Gloucestershire must be ready for cutting but it did not. His thoughts were centred on Martha: her sudden departure could have been foreseen, if only he had thought about it more deeply, and he reproached himself for not having called more often at Rydd House, in spite of being unwelcome there, while he wondered what had been the final cause of her going.

His mother had the explanation on the tip of her tongue. Miss Lingford was jealous of her younger sister and had not been willing to hand over the reins to her. Drum did not agree: there was no jealousy in Martha.

He left next day for London and called at the Angel in St. Clements where the Tonbridge coach had set her down, and after making enquiries there he found a chambermaid who remembered a young lady travelling alone on the day in question, without a maid too, which seemed strange because few young ladies travelled stage without taking servants with them. This young lady had kept herself to herself: she did not even complain of the bugs although having engaged one of the cheapest rooms she must have been kept awake by them all night.

"Did she say where she was going?" asked Mr. Connington.

At first the girl said she did not know, and he fancied she was suspicious of him, perhaps afraid that he had designs upon Martha and that the young lady had run away from him for her own good, but when he produced a guinea to help her memory she concluded that he was a very nice gentleman, after all, and told him that she thought the lady must have been going to Bath because she had booked a place on the mail for the following morning.

Of course, he thought, the young Lingfords had relatives in Bath, the good Honeymans. They had been visiting them when he had first met them. He left the Angel that night, taking his new horses and his carriage down the Bath road in the moonshine and arriving at that queen of cities early in the morning two days later.

Once there he realized that before he called on Mr. Honeyman he must take stock of himself and his own feelings and discover what he was doing there, pursuing Martha Lingford across England, and why.

The answers to these questions resolved themselves into only one: his interest had never been so deeply stirred over any woman before and he could not rest until he knew that she was safe.

The little house in Crome seemed much smaller than Martha remembered it, and although her aunt welcomed her with her usual kindness she could see that she was not happy at her decision to leave her grandfather.

"Don't you think it a little unwise, dearest, to act on a sudden impulse?"

Martha assured her that it had not been a sudden impulse at all: it was a decision taken during the time that Sukey had been away making the acquaintance of her husband's relations who were already in England. "There are some in London, others in Surrey and at least two families in Hertfordshire," she added, "so that she had a round of visits to make before she came home. And from the start my grandfather and I disliked each other. It is very fortunate that he has taken such a fancy to Sukey. She and Charles are now safely off my hands." She smiled reassuringly at Miss Honeyman. "All that remains is for me to find some way of earning my bread."

"My dearest child, you cannot do that!" Her aunt was horrified. "What can you do?"

"I can teach French. Oh, I know I cannot chatter away in the language as Sukey does, but I can teach the grammar and translation, though not with a very good accent I'm afraid."

"You have a beautiful French accent, dear," protested her aunt, who had never been able to learn French in her life.

"And I can teach the use of the globes," continued Martha cheerfully, "and the pence table, and dancing, and plain sewing as well as embroidery stitches—broad stitch, cross and changes—and I can teach drawing and painting and the cutting of paper and playing on the pianoforte. Except that I have no pianoforte now! I see no reason though why I should not hire a room in a decent house in Crome and set up a school for young ladies here."

"But what will you do for servants, my love?" I am very vexed that Betsy did not come with you."

"I am very glad that she did not. And here are all the servants I shall need, Aunt Deb." She held out her hands and laughed at Miss Honeyman's shocked expression. "Helped of course by two willing feet! Come, Aunt Debbie, I still have nearly fifty pounds left. I am sure I can start a school with that."

"There is the parlour upstairs that overlooks the street," said her aunt hopefully. "You can make a start there if you liked, Martha dearest, I never use it because it is too large to heat properly in the cold weather."

"I believe you mean that." Martha came to her and kissed her. "I promise you that if I cannot find anything within my means then I shall be very pleased to start my school in your lovely parlour upstairs."

So it was arranged, and every morning over the next week Martha went out to look for a house for her school. It would scarcely be an establishment based on the refined academy in Bath where Sukey had been taught French and dancing and little else beside: for her pupils she aimed no higher than the daughters of the tradesmen in Crome. Her quest proved to be disappointing, however. There were several houses that would have suited her purpose admirably had the owners been content to let her rent only the rooms she required, but most wished to let the whole house. And the houses with large rooms were too expensive while the cheaper ones were far too small.

At last however she found a house in a paved walk not far from the church, where two small rooms above had already been made into one. The uneven oak floor was suitable for dancing lessons and the windows were sufficiently large to throw light into the room for the scholars to see their work.

"I will have a blackboard there," she thought, "at the far end. And a table beside it. And here the globe and seats for the children round the table." Her school began to materialize in her mind, and as it did so for the first time since she left Rydd doubts began to assail her.

How much should she charge for instance? Certainly not as much as the establishment in Bath with its French mademoiselle, its dancing master, its drawing and music masters. And how long would her fifty pounds last, after she had bought chairs and the table and the blackboard and the globe, and paid a quarter's rent in advance for her school?

She crossed the room and stared disconsolately at the houses on the opposite side, and as she did so a man came down the walk under the window and after a moment's hesitation knocked, and then walked in at the door that she had left on the latch. This, she thought unhappily, must be the owner of the house come to know her decision. He had told her that his sister was anxious to remove there from Bath if she decided against it. But Aunt Deb was right: it was useless to hurry into such an enterprise without more thought.

With her father's errors returning vividly to her mind as the gentleman entered the room behind her, she said without turning her head, "I am sorry, sir but this house is beyond my means. I am afraid I cannot agree to take it."

"I am glad to hear it," said a familiar voice and she whirled round.

"You!" she exclaimed, her face showing her chagrin. "What in Heaven's name are you doing in Crome, Mr. Connington?"

"I have been looking for you," he said mildly. He came and joined her in the window above the paved lane, leaning against the folded shutters and studying her angry face as if he found it very satisfactory to see it there, unwelcoming as it was.

"My grandfather sent you," she accused him and her eyes sparkled. "Very well. You will please to go back to him without loss of time, Mr. Connington, and tell him that nothing he can do or say will make me return to Rydd House. I never want to see that house, or the wicked old man in it, again. I would sooner starve."

"I am also delighted to hear you say that," said Drum and went on conversationally, "Your grandfather of course had nothing to do with it, so stop scolding, Martha and listen to me. I went to your uncle and aunt in Bath directly I arrived, and I had to be circumspect because I did not know how much had been revealed to them of your reason for leaving Rydd so suddenly. At first they said they knew nothing of your whereabouts, but after dinner at their house one evening, while the ladies were waiting for us to join them for tea and coffee in the drawing-room, your uncle became somewhat mellowed with some excellent French brandy, and he told me the whole story as you had told it to your aunt, Miss Honeyman, and she in turn had related it to your aunt in Bath. He also said that you had behaved as an angel to those two youngsters and that Miss Sukey was always a vain, spoilt little piece, and he did not wonder that she had turned on you in the finish."

"But—" The anger died a little in her face and her eyes softened and he thought he saw a flicker of a smile on her mouth. "If you did not come from my grandfather, why did you come? Because you were bored?"

But he had never been bored since he had known her. "I came on my own account," he said. "Because I love you and I want to marry you. Will you marry me, Martha?" It came so easily, so naturally, that he knew it must have been in his mind from the day when he first saw her with her uncle outside the print-shop in Bath.

She had opened her mouth to tell him about her school but the words remained unuttered. "*What* did you say?" she asked.

He repeated his statement, and drawled, "I am quite aware that you do not love me, but you might come to it in time."

In the shadowed room, darkened by the houses opposite that were almost near enough to touch, her astonishment changed to controlled impatience, while her hazel eyes studied him half despairing, half amused.

"I have long suspected," she told him, "that under an affectation of boredom you are one of the kindest men on earth and now I am sure of it. You followed me because you thought I might be feeling in need of help, so you have made this chivalrous—if unwise—offer, which I will relieve your mind by telling you I do not mean to accept. I have decided to start a little school for young ladies here in Crome. I know a great deal about the management of young ladies—not quite enough yet, perhaps, but with more experience I shall do very well"—she broke off.

"You will do no such thing," he said. "You will not look after any more young ladies, because they are an ungrateful lot, and it is time that somebody looked after you." Gently he put his hands on her shoulders and turned her face towards himself. "You look sad," he said. "Have I added to your troubles, Martha my love, when I only wanted to alleviate them?"

She shook her head. "I am a very independent woman, Mr. Connington," she said firmly. "I like to stand on my own feet."

"Women have no right to be independent." He frowned and his hands dropped to his sides. "Martha, start your little school if you must, but I am not going to give up. I shall come back again and again, until one day when your young ladies have been exceptionally trying and stupid and teasing—as another young lady has been recently—I shall come as usual and I shall say, '*Now* will you marry me?' And you will say—quite meekly—'Yes, please, Drum, I will.' So

you might as well say it at once and save us both
a great deal of time. And what is more I shall be freed
from the necessity of journeying to Crome frequently
from Arcott, which I shall find a dead bore."

But she only laughed at him and shook her head
again and said she thought she would go back to her
aunt's house and measure up the size of the large
parlour upstairs. He left for Gloucestershire early on
the following day.

But after his visit a correspondence began between
them in a somewhat cool fashion. Martha began it by
thanking him, as she thought only civil, for the offer
he had made her.

Dear Mr. Connington
  *While I cannot believe that you meant what you
said, I am certain when you have had time to think
it over you will be relieved that I had the prudence
not to take you seriously. I hope you will be happy to
learn that my school is to open next Monday with six
pupils—the butcher's two daughters and the first four
of the baker's dozen. Sincerely, M. Lingford.*

His reply came swiftly:

Dear Martha
  *I was serious, I do not admire excessive prudence,
and I am not happy to know that you have a school of
six small girls. Confusion to them! I will visit Crome
at the end of this month. Your devoted Drum.*

Her next letter was written after this second visit of
his that August.

Dear Mr. Connington,
  *My aunt wishes me to convey her thanks for the
ducks and the side of smoked bacon you brought on*

your last visit to her, but I feel I must protest at this second journey of yours to Crome. It is a long way from Arcott Manor. I am sorry I did not see more of you while you were here but I was occupied with my pupils. Sincerely, M. Lingford.

His answer came even more swiftly than the other:

My dearest Martha,
As you resolutely refused to remove that hideous cap of yours and come downstairs to talk to me, I was forced to throw myself upon the mercy of your aunt, whom I found delightful. We had long and interesting conversations and I was glad to learn that you have a liking of apricots. I intend to plant a tree on a south wall this autumn, and I have promised Miss Honeyman a rose tree which I will plant myself beside her front gate. You will be able to see it from your schoolroom window and it may remind you of me. Your devoted Drum.

"That man!" Martha exploded with wrath when she read it. "Will nothing persuade him that I am serious?"

"I do not think so, dearest." Miss Honeyman was serene. "He is a most charming man. I promise you that if I were your cousin instead of your aunt you would not stand a chance. I would cut you out as sure as my name is Deborah Honeyman. I love him already."

"What do you talk about when I am not there?" asked Martha curiously.

"About you, and his house in Gloucestershire, and about you again, and how we both dislike independence in women."

Martha said she must go and unpick some embroidery that had been disgracefully done by one of her pupils.

At the end of September Drum Connington's carriage

was once more in front of Miss Honeyman's gate, and his servant carried in a small rose tree with its roots wrapped in sacking, besides a leash of partridges, a couple of hares and another side of smoked bacon.

Miss Honeyman greeted Mr. Connington with affection, calling him her dear Drum and offering her cheek for his kiss. Martha looked on frowning, and when she held out her hand to him in greeting her smile was frosty. But he noticed that she had removed her cap and it reassured him a little. He told her that he had planted his apricot tree and it appeared to be thriving. "I believe apricots thrive in the Gloucestershire air," he remarked, "if they are protected from cold winds."

"I like apricots,' she told him tartly, "because they have a stringency akin to my temper."

"That is my opinion exactly," he assured her and left her with nothing to say. He refused to share the partridges with them, having ordered his dinner at the Bull, and the next morning he solemnly planted the rose tree by the gate. Once more he renewed his offer of marriage before he left and she refused him somewhat brusquely. Later however, when they were enjoying slices of the excellent bacon that had been smoked at Arcott she felt she might have hurt him by her brusqueness and she wrote to him in a gentler mood:

Dear Mr. Connington
  I must beg your pardon for not having spared you more of my time when you had come so far, and brought my aunt such welcome additions to her larder, but you must blame my unlucky temper. I have a character that I fear you would not like if you came to know it better. You may be pleased to know that I have two more pupils, starting next Monday. Sincerely Martha Lingford.

"Come," he said, smiling a little as he read it, "we are progressing, I believe—if only at an inch at a time."

He wrote in reply: *Dearest Martha, I am not pleased to learn that you have two more pupils. I detest small girls. Drum.*

She missed the words "Your devoted" and thought she detected anger and impatience in the short letter. She wrote back in haste: *Dear Drum, My two new pupils are boys. Martha.*

Which made him laugh and reply: *Dearest Martha, Damn all small boys. Purchase a birch rod and do not spare it. Drum.*

She did not reply and at the end of October he was in Crome again, with a bushel of apples from the Arcott orchards and a hindquarter of veal, and she tried to unbend a little and then was afraid she was encouraging him and stiffened. Her aunt despaired of her, but Drum told her not to worry. "She will have me in the end," he said with more conviction perhaps than he felt.

"I wish I could be as sure. You are very devoted, Drum.'"

"I am confoundedly in love with her, ma'am." After a pause he added: "In fact I love her so much that I cannot think that she will not have me."

Miss Honeyman put out a hand to him. "Dear Drum! Stupid, stupid girl!"

"No." He took her hand in his with a warm pressure. "She has been deeply hurt through Sukey—whom she loved and trusted. She has to learn to love and trust again and it will take time." A sudden thunderous noise from the room above interrupted him: a bumping and jumping and stamping that brought him to his feet. "What the devil is that?" he demanded in alarm. "Are her pupils attacking her?"

"No." Miss Honeyman laughed. "They have no fire in the room—it has been such mild weather, you know—and she is afraid that the children may get chilled. So every now and then she makes them leave their lessons and teaches them country dances—to warm them up."

"And to bring your ceiling down, ma'am!"

Miss Honeyman glanced up at her ceiling with a smile. "It has stood up for a number of years and I daresay it will stand up for a number of years more," she said with a placidity that was somewhat disturbed by a louder bump than usual that made the ornaments on the parlour chimney-piece jump about in harmony. "Boys are so rough," she said with a small sigh. "I wish she had kept to girls."

When Drum said goodbye on Monday morning she begged him not come during the winter months. "We are usually snowed up here," she said. "And I am sure it is as bad in Gloucestershire."

"Lord bless you yes. Last winter my people had to dig through snow four feet deep to reach the turnpike." He glanced up the stairs to the schoolroom door which was firmly shut, and then he put a box of Tunbridge ware into her hands. "It is locked," he pointed out, "and here is the key, which I would advise you to keep on a ribbon round your neck."

"Why? What is in it?" The blue eyes were wider than ever.

"That is to be a secret between you and me, ma'am.

There is a letter inside, but when you have read it I beg you will not reveal its contents to anybody."

"Not even to Martha?"

"Especially not to Martha."

After he had gone she took the little box to her room and opened it and read the letter. It was very short, asking her to use the contents for Martha's school and all other expenses she might incur. There was beneath the letter a purse containing one hundred guineas. That afternoon there also arrived at Miss Honeyman's house so large a load of logs that after the woodshed was filled they had to be stored in the cellar. "The gentleman said they was to stop your ceiling from falling down, ma'am," said the carter, much mystified and was more mystified still when Miss Honeyman laughed.

That time Mr. Connington left without making an offer to Martha and after she had watched him go from her window and acknowledged the farewell flourish of his hat with a cool bow she worried about it. Certainly she had given him little opportunity when they were alone together, but he was not a man to waste his opportunities, however slight. From her window she could see that the rose tree had shed its last leaves but it appeared to be flourishing, and she wondered how the apricot was progressing before turning back with a sigh to keep order in her noisy little class.

Drum did not come in November, leaving his next visit to a week before Christmas, when he arrived with a goose, another bushel of apples, a score or so of eggs and a sack of white flour, which was becoming difficult to buy in Crome owing to the war. These contributions to her table came as a god-send to Miss

Honeyman, as Charles had arrived the day before and she had been wondering how she should be able to satisfy the appetite he had brought with him.

Charles said that Sukey seemed surprised to learn that her sister had started a school in their aunt's house in Crome. "I concluded you had not told her," he added.

"No," said Martha. "There was no reason for me to do so."

"I came away," Charles went on, "because I could not stomach all those French relatives of de Salle's at Rydd House."

"Why, are they many of them there?" asked Martha.

"They fill it from attic to cellar," said Charles in disgust. "Grandfather calls it Juniper Hall. That is a house in Surrey," he explained to Miss Honeyman, "where a whole lot of *émigrés* live—you might call it a French colony."

"And how does Betsy get on with them?"

"She does not like them at all. She refuses to make any shirts for Jules."

"It sounds as if she is getting lazy."

"Oh, she makes my shirts and Grandfather's," said Charles easily. "And do you know, she hid my pistols in her room 'in case they Frenchies get them'. I have them with me in my trunk."

"Dear Betsy." Martha asked with some constraint after their grandfather.

"He shuts himself up in his little room and only comes out to take the head of the table at dinner. The French people don't like him very much because he smokes a pipe of tobacco after his dinner, and he don't like the Frenchmen because they use scent."

Charles wrinkled his nose in disgust. "Even their pomade is scented! Faugh!"

Mr. Connington's arrival on the following day needed an explanation and he gave it with his most languid drawl. He was on his way to Kent for Christmas and thought he would call in at Crome on the way, and if Charles thought it was an odd way to reach Kent from Gloucestershire he was too polite and too much in awe of Mr. Connington to say so.

The next day as Martha was on her way upstairs to her pupils she saw her brother in the hall with his topcoat on and he told her with great delight that Drum had promised to show him how to handle his four-in-hand. "But I daresay he will not let me drive them of course," he added wistfully.

"I daresay he will not too. Why, Charles, Mr. Connington will not allow his own coachman to handle his teams of horses if he can avoid it."

"No, I suppose he would not." As they made their way out of the town a little later behind Mr. Connington's fine horses their owner asked politely after the new Marquise de Salle, but Charles dismissed Sukey in a few words and was more eager to relate Captain Redfern's latest exploit.

"A boat put into the harbour for one night," he told his companion. "She was the size of the *Turk*—if you remember her sir. The *Turk* was the boat that fetched Jules and his family to Rydd."

"I remember her," said Drum.

"Well, it appears that Captain Redfern swore that this boat was the *Turk* disguised—she had the name *Tiger* painted on her hull—and he wasn't the only one. Old Amos was certain she was the *Turk*, and Amos knows every boat on sight. I don't know why the *Turk* should have come into the harbour in that way, mind you, when nobody had set eyes on her for months, but at all events Captain Redfern had it that she had been smuggling on a large scale since she left Rydd and when she slipped out of harbour he gave chase and signalled to her to heave to, and then, as her master took no notice, he overhauled her and she had the impudence to open her guns on the *Snipe*. So Captain Redfern replied with a broadside and sank her. And it *was* the *Turk*."

"Indeed?" Mr. Connington seemed more interested in his off-leader's ears. "And what happened to the crew? Were they drowned?"

"Only the master—a man by the name of Adam Dury. He never learned to swim, saying that he preferred to drown quickly. The others were saved but it is thought they will be let off."

Having reached the open road Mr. Connington lost interest in Rydd and began to give his young friend his first lesson in the art of controlling four spirited horses at a time. That afternoon Charles returned in great delight, because on a straight bit of road with not even a horseman in sight, he had been allowed to handle the reins for fifteen minutes, and what was more Drum had told him he had the makings of a good driver.

"You know, as we were coming home," Charles went on seriously "it occurred to me that Mr. Connington might be interested in you, Martha."

"Oh?" His sister began to make up the parlour fire, not daring to look at her aunt. "What ever could have given you such a notion, Charles?"

"He talked about you a great deal," said Charles. "For a man like Mr. Connington it seemed odd to me —almost as if he were as interested in you as he was in his horses. If you could see your way to not wearing a cap and to having your hair dressed and—pinking —and that sort of thing, I daresay he might even make you an offer before going on to Kent."

Miss Honeyman left the room abruptly and Martha turned from making up the fire, poker in hand, her eyes sparkling and her cheeks flushed. "Has he been asking you to talk to me about it?" she demanded.

"Of course not. How you do flare up at a fellow! I told you it is entirely my own idea."

"Then I will tell you at once Charles that Mr. Connington has made me an offer and I have refused him."

"You refused him?" Charles could not believe it. "But Martha—"

"I know Mr. Connington rather better than you do, my dear," his sister told him. "He is a most kind and generous man, and his offer was inspired by chivalry. If I married him he would soon repent of his bargain and wish he had married a woman more fitted to his way of life."

"But do you dislike him then?"

"I do not dislike him at all."

"Then why—if he is such a good fellow, and I believe you there—the way he handles those horses of his I shall never forget—why if you do not dislike him, do you not marry him and risk him repenting? After all," went on Charles philosophically, "I daresay most couples repent of having married each other after a time."

"They should not," said Martha slowly.

"But he is so rich Martha—and there's Arcott—"

"That has nothing to do with it," said Martha firmly. "So let us discuss it no more."

"*Women!*" said Charles in disgust.

The following morning however Drum Connington had something more to say about it before he left for Kent.

Having found Martha in the parlour without her cap—she had given her pupils a holiday during the remainder of Charles's stay—he prolonged his leave-taking until Miss Honeyman removed Charles and his chat about Mr. Connington's horses to her larder, to pick out some of the apples he wished to take back with him to Portsmouth, leaving his sister with her wealthy suitor.

Yet now that they were alone together Drum seemed preoccupied and not inclined to linger, and just before Miss Honeyman and Charles returned he said abruptly: "I conclude that you have not changed your mind, Martha?"

"No." She felt suddenly conscience-stricken. "Mr. Connington, will you not be sensible over this and believe me when I tell you that I mean what I say? Persistence can become . . ." She hesitated.

"A dead bore," he finished for her. "I beg your pardon. You dislike me and I could not believe it. My vanity has been at fault and I will persist no longer."

He took her hand in his, smiled down at her a little sadly, and then the others came back and he made his farewells and went away, his fine carriage causing all the small boys of the neighbourhood to race after it shouting as he went.

Sixteen

January passed without a word from Drum Connington and without a visit. It was a hard winter and Martha drew a bleak comfort from the thought that the roads were impassable, not only for private coaches but for the mails, and that she could not expect Drum to take his fine horses through fifty miles of bitter weather for the sake of a young woman who had been as ungracious as she had at their last meeting.

When February passed too without a letter from Arcott she wondered if at last he had taken her at her word and intended to have no more to do with her, and most unreasonably the possibility dismayed her utterly. She clung to the hope that he would visit them in March, although when that boisterous month came in like a lion, with gales ripping through the trees with a

213

noise like thunder, and the rain turning innocent little streams into raging torrents overnight, it did not seem that hope would be realized. She counted the days until the quieter weather came, but Drum did not come with it: instead, at the beginning of April a letter arrived from his mother, addressed to Miss Honeyman and seeming to bring with it the end of their acquaintance with her son.

Lady Connington had not approved of writing the letter at all.

"Miss Honeyman!" she exclaimed. "Who is she, pray, that she is so important?"

"A lady, Mamma."

"Is she a young lady?"

"I never know if a lady wishes to be thought young or old."

"Honeyman." Her ladyship frowned. "Is she related to the people of the same name in Bath?"

"She is Mr. Honeyman's sister I believe."

"Then she has no money because Fanny told me he had none before he married. Do you know what her income is?"

"I have not been discourteous enough to enquire."

His mother checked a discourteous remark herself by asking what he wished her to say to Miss Honeyman.

"Simply that in encountering a loaded London wagon in a narrow road I got the worst of the bargain and was thrown over a hedge, breaking my right arm, so that I am unable to write to her myself. But tell her that directly I am able to hold the reins and control my cattle I shall be with her in Somerset."

"So that is the lady you have been constantly visit-

THE TEMPESTUOUS PETTICOAT   215

ing in Somerset throughout last summer!" cried his
mamma.

"You have been talking to Mrs. Hurst," he accused
her and saw her blush. "My housekeeper is the biggest
gossip in the country besides having the brain of a
hen. There was no need for her to send off post-haste
for you. A broken arm is not a broken back dammit."

"Is there anything else you wish me to tell the
lady?" asked his mother coldly.

"I would like you to send my regards to her niece,
Miss Lingford," said her son with deceptive mildness.

"Miss Lingford!" Light suddenly dawned. "That hoyden! I conclude she is the Miss Lingford who was
visiting her grandfather in Rydd recently?"

"The same."

"And now that she has quarrelled with the old man
and her sister no doubt she has been doing her best to
entrap you down there in Somerset. Abominable girl!
I never thought that you, Drum—so fastidious, so hard
to please—could allow yourself to be duped by a young
woman of her character."

"I would beg you, ma'am, to take care how you
speak of a lady whom I am endeavouring to make your
daughter." There was no drawl now in Drum's voice
and the expression in his eyes frightened her a little.
She said quickly:

"You have had a few mistresses, my dear. I did not
think you contemplated a more serious tie with Miss
Lingford."

"I would not dare suggest anything else." The drawl
came back maddeningly. "If I did she would probably
box my ears or shoot me."

"You will never take anything seriously," complained Lady Connington.

"Nevertheless you will write that letter for me and see that it is taken to the post office?"

"Yes," she said, "I will write your letter, Drum, and it shall be taken to the post office today."

The letter however was vastly different from the one he had asked her to write.

Dear Miss Honeyman, she wrote, *My Son, Mr. Meldrum Connington, had a bad Mishap with his Horses a few weeks ago, suffering many Broken Bones. When I received his house-keeper's letter summoning me to Arcott I set off at once from Kent, and our Friend Miss Racksby would have accompanied me had not her Father promised to bring her later, when we Knew how serious the Injuries might be and what chance there may be of Recovery. As my son no doubt has told you—Being an Old Acquaintance—we are all Hoping that Miss Racksby will become something nearer than a Friend in the Future. I am sure I regard Her as my Daughter already. The Friends of a man in Mr. Meldrum Connington's Position expect him to marry a Lady of Consequence and Leonora is a great Favorite with us All. I trust your niece does well with her School? My mantua-maker's daughter teaches in a school in Salisbury I believe. Sincerely yours, S. Connington.*

Miss Honeyman read the letter in silence before handing it to Martha to read and watched her face go white.

Was this why he had avoided them before this mishap she wondered, because he had at last turned for consolation to Miss Racksby? And how badly was he hurt?

Her aunt studied the letter for a second time while

Martha attempted to conduct her school with her mind anywhere but on her pupils, and it seemed to Miss Honeyman that there was something that needed explanation in her ladyship's effusion. Why, for instance had she written? It must have been because Drum had asked her to write: how else would she have known how to address her letter? She did not believe one word about Miss Racksby, she decided at last: had not Drum told her himself that he was "confoundedly" in love with Martha, and she did not think even in the face of Martha's persistent refusals that he would have forgotten her so soon. But because he had asked his mother to write to her it pointed to the mishap as being serious enough to prevent him from writing himself. There was the chance that parts of the letter might be true therefore and that he might be very seriously injured indeed, that in fact he might die, and that was a threat that she could not ignore.

Sitting there by the parlour fire worrying about it she remembered the Tunbridge ware box: they would use some of its contents to travel to Gloucestershire themselves and discover the extent of dear Drum's injuries and nobody should stop them. If they travelled post they could arrive within a day.

At dinnertime she told Martha's pupils that urgent family business had called her and Miss Lingford away from home, and she handed each child a three-corner note to give to their parents. When the children had scampered back upstairs Martha stayed behind to protest.

"Aunt Deb," she said, "we cannot go to Arcott— you know we cannot. What excuse can we give to Lady Connington? And besides—Miss Racksby and her father may be there by this time."

"I do not mind my dear if a dozen Miss Racksbys and their fathers are there," said Miss Honeyman serenely. "And Lady Connington will not be able to prevent two old friends of Drum's from calling to enquire how he does. We will travel post, Martha, I have made up my mind to that. If we leave the house at seven we should have covered the fifty miles to Arcott by the end of the day. Annie shall step round to her mother this afternoon to see if she is able to come in and keep her company while we are away."

Martha stared at her little aunt in astonishment. Never in all the years she had known her had Miss Honeyman taken charge of a situation with such determination, and in spite of herself her heart lifted a little. As she turned towards the stairs after her pupils her aunt added, "When your class is finished my love, you must pack what you will need. And may I beg you to wear your cloak with its becoming hood, and not that dreadful hat?"

When they started out the next morning, however, Miss Honeyman's anxiety over Drum showed itself in urging the post-boys to go faster.

"I always thought post-chaises flew along," she told Martha indignantly. "You would think so when you see them tearing through Crome. But this one has crawled." As they started out again she once more urged the post-boy—a surly man—to hurry, and he replied by asking her if she wanted his horses to drop dead.

Martha did not know if she wanted the horses to hurry or to be slow. She could only think of life without Drum, without his warm smile at the sight of her, even when she was wearing her hideous cap or her more deplorable hat. She thought of his voice, drawlingly declaring his boredom, of his readiness to endure her unkindness, and the thought came to her that if he recovered sufficiently to marry Leonora Racksby she had only herself to blame. And yet, as she had pointed out to Charles, how could she take advantage of his chivalry?

The miles passed, Miss Honeyman complaining bitterly that the toll-gates appeared to be manned by imbeciles, and that she could not see why they must wait two hours for horses to be baited when there were no fresh ones available, but they arrived at Ainswick at last and knew that they were only five miles from Arcott Manor. It was ten o'clock and dark when they entered the little town, but with the light from the lamps over gateways and in the windows they recognized it from Drum's description. A charming little town, he had called it, with a welcoming air. Certainly the landlord of the Green Man welcomed them kindly as they stepped from their chaise, glad to ease their cramped limbs after the day's travel. They had decided between them to sleep the night at the inn rather than travel on to Arcott, and as they waited for beds to be prepared for them Miss Honeyman enquired of the landlord if he had any news of Mr. Meldrum Connington.

"We understood that he had been badly injured in a mishap with the horses," she said, while Martha stood silently beside her, gripping her hands together under her cloak.

"Bless you yes, ma'am, he wur thrown over a hedge," said the landlord cheerfully. "But he's recovered now.

'Er laddyship wur here two days ago on her way to Kent, and she say he wur mending fast."

"I am very glad to hear that," said Miss Honeyman with a glance at her niece whose face registered a deep but somewhat puzzled relief. While they waited for supper to be brought to them before they retired to bed Martha remarked with a return to her old firmness that there was no need to worry any more over Drum, and they would start their journey back to Somerset the next morning.

Miss Honeyman nearly burst into tears. She even felt unkindly that it was a pity Mr. Connington had been so little injured as if he had been worse they would have had every excuse to visit him on the following day. As they ate their supper Martha explained that she was not ungrateful.

"But now that he is recovered, dearest Aunt Deb, you must see for yourself that it would scarcely be proper for us to pursue him any further."

Miss Honeyman began to wish that they had not come at all. In the morning however, after a sound night's sleep, Martha allowed herself to be persuaded that it would be only courteous to pay a morning call on Mr. Connington on their way home.

They started out through a countryside that was just stirring after a long winter's sleep. Primroses were out in the banks on the sunny side of the roads, and in the wide expanse of sky over the Cotwolds sunshine was chasing rain clouds and sending shadows racing over the landscape into the blue mists of the horizon.

Arcott was a small honey-coloured manor house, built round a square courtyard, with slates of stone where lichen grew to add to their beauty. Farm buildings stood a little distance away across the fields, and cattle and sheep were grazing in a little park surrounded by drystone walls.

The chaise stopped before a porch in the courtyard and the doors within it opened and servants came out to help them from the carriage and to conduct them into the house.

No, they said in answer to Martha's anxious enquiries, there were no guests staying at the Manor: Mr. Connington was quite alone.

They followed them through a square hall to where a door opened off it into a library, where Drum was seated by a cheerful fire reading a newspaper. Except for having his right arm in a sling he looked remarkably well. His astonishment at seeing them was only equalled by his delight, and he welcomed them warmly to Arcott.

Hastily Martha explained about the letter. "Poor Aunt Deb received a letter from your mother last Monday that frightened her most dreadfully with an account of your mishap with your carriage. From what her ladyship said we imagined you to be at death's door —and so—because Aunt Deb was so anxious about you—we travelled to Ainswick yesterday to find out how you did. We were very pleased to learn from the landlord that her ladyship's concern for you had exaggerated the gravity of your condition."

He asked if Miss Honeyman had brought the letter with her and she produced it from her reticule for him to read.

"This is preposterous!" he exclaimed when he had done. "I apologize, Miss Honeyman, for my mother's habit of exaggeration, which this time has passed all bounds. Have I your permission to destroy this?"

"Of course, Drum dear." Miss Honeyman smiled happily as he dropped the offending letter into the heart of the fire.

"The only bone I broke was in my right arm, confound it," he told them. "It meant that I was unable to hold a pen—or worse still—hold the reins. I asked my mother to write to assure you that I should be in Somerset again directly I could control my horses."

He sent for refreshments and as they ate and drank he asked Miss Honeyman if, now she had come so far, she would not be persuaded to take pity on him and stay at Arcott for a week at least before returning to Crome.

"You see before you, Miss Honeyman, a man almost dead from boredom with his own company, and I have only to tell my housekeeper to prepare rooms for you and it will be done." He dare not look at Martha as he continued quickly, "I am sure you must be in need of a rest."

Miss Honeyman admitted that she felt extremely fatigued and Drum took it as settled. The housekeeper was summoned and Miss Honeyman departed with her thankfully to rest a little while before dinner, while servants were despatched to bring the ladies' luggage in from the carriage, and the chaise was dismissed and the post-boys paid off with all Drum's usual déspatch.

He returned happily to the library where he found Martha at the window that looked on to a side lawn where a small apricot tree was showing signs of bursting into bloom against a south wall.

"I am sorry my mamma wrote as she did," he said.

"I had no notion she would alarm—Miss Honeyman —so much, or I would have waited until I could write the letter myself. But I have never been clever with my left hand and I could not hold a pen." He glanced at her unresponsive back and went on with a wry little smile, "It would have been vastly more romantic had you found me on my death-bed, like the heroes of the novels my mamma likes to read, but I am no hero, Martha, as I fear you have discovered, and in the irritating way I have I am extremely well."

"Why will you laugh at me?" she asked in a low voice, and the apricot tree was suddenly dimmed by a mist of tears.

"I beg your pardon, I did not mean to laugh at you my dear." He studied her frowning, trying to make up his mind. One false move now and he might lose her for ever. And then she went on quietly:

"Your mother was right, Drum. In your position you should marry a woman of consequence."

"Of consequence to whom? To the world or to me?" He joined her in the window. "Martha my dear, let's make an end of it, shall we?"

She turned quickly and caught her breath, and he saw the tears on her lashes and took heart. "An— end?" she repeated.

"Yes. Here is my hand. You have only to take it, to look me in the face and to tell me that you cannot love me and that you will never marry me, and I swear I will plague you no more. The whole question of marriage between us will never be mentioned again and you will be free to return to your horrid little girls and your naughty little boys in peace."

It was a prospect that no longer held the slightest attraction for her.

"After your kindness and goodness to me," she said unsteadily, "and my unkindness and badness to you, I find it difficult to believe that you can still love me."

"Have you any real doubt of it? Martha, my lovely tempestuous petticoat, will you have me?"

The moment in a dark little house in Crome was back with her again. She took his hand in hers and held it against her cheek and over it her eyes, half-mischievous and wholly tender, met his. "Yes, if you please, Drum," she said.

There appeared to be no more need for polite conversation between them. His uninjured arm came round her and he drew her close and kissed her, and then as she raised not the smallest objection, he kissed her again.

Outside, snugly protected against the cold wind by its south wall, the little apricot tree opened its first blossom full into the April sun.